Ju  **ow she** ... **bones.**

...sa froze, instinct ta... ...r.

...en he leaned toward her, slowly, as if he didn't
...nt to frighten her. "Don't move," he whispered.

...didn't think she could have, at least not at that
...ent. Was he about to drink from her?

...hands cupped her cheeks. His skin was cool and
...oth, smoother than human flesh. Jude touched
... mouth with his. A light touch. His lips were
...ted, and he inhaled, taking her breath into him.
... sighed, and she felt the coolness of his breath
... an autumn breeze.

...en he kissed her.

Dear Reader,

What would a vampire fear more than dying permanently? Like most of you, I've read Bram Stoker and Anne Rice, and some other tales about vampires. The myth continues to evolve.

But I got to wondering: This change to being undead and surviving on blood, what would it do to a person if it really happened? Would need kill conscience? And what in the world would cause a vampire more fear than the thought of dying permanently?

Out of that came Jude Messenger, vampire private investigator and demon slayer. Jude not only fights the evil of the night, but he battles himself as well. Then he meets Terri, a rather independent medical examiner who drives him nearly insane with needs he has long battled, and worse, she puts him in danger of the thing vampires fear more than permanent death: The Claiming.

Hugs,

Rachel

Rachel Lee was hooked on writing by the age of twelve, and practiced her craft as she moved from place to place all over the United States. This *New York Times* bestselling author now resides in Florida and has the joy of writing full-time.

Rachel Lee was hooked on writing by the age of twelve, and practiced her craft as she moved from place to place all over the United States. This New York Times bestselling author now resides in Florida and has the joy of writing full-time.

Chapter 1

He smelled her long before he saw her. A sweet, luscious smell wafted to him on the breeze, the kind of scent that raised his hunger to dangerous levels. He paused for a moment, invisible in the dark shadow of a building on a nighttime street dotted only infrequently with the yellow of street lamps.

He gave himself some time to drink in the intoxicating scent, a few moments of masochistic torture because he knew he wouldn't heed the siren call to feed. He'd stopped heeding that call a long time ago, except for an occasional, harmless but necessary half-pint.

Besides, he had found those willing to share, a few trustworthy humans who would allow him to feed in exchange for the sexual thrill.

But this scent called to him, as only a few had over the centuries. He lifted his head, drinking it in, forgetting for a few seconds that he had work to do, a job to complete. For just a few seconds he allowed himself to remember how it had once been when he'd hunted freely, merely to satisfy himself.

Then he shook himself out of the hunger, and closed off his needs. He had changed, times had changed, and practice made control easier, though no less painful.

The job, he reminded himself. The address was only two blocks away. He moved freely, shadow to shadow, with a speed that would make him nearly invisible to all but the most perceptive. In this part of town there were no crowds to mingle with and thus hide among. The warehouse district was almost deserted and at night, only those with evil in mind dared to emerge after darkness claimed the street.

Evil had brought him here.

He was still half a block away from his target when he smelled the intoxicating scent again. But this time it was even more compelling because now it definitely held an overtone of fear.

And fear was another siren call for his kind, a part he had come to loathe.

He paused, torn. The evil he had come to deal with or the evil he sensed about to happen?

A woman's cry pierced the night, making his decision for him. Forgetting the shadows for speed, he dashed toward the sound, the scent, moving now at a speed that rendered him invisible to human eyes.

Three blocks to the east he found her. She stood surrounded by four punks, one of them holding a knife, every single one of them looking as if they enjoyed frightening her as much as one of his kind might. He could smell their evil intentions. And something else. Something he couldn't identify, but it disturbed him.

"Don't touch me," she demanded, taking an aggressive posture, as if she was willing to attack *them*. Little good it would do when she was outnumbered. "Don't. Take my money. Take my credit cards."

"Hey, sweetie," said the guy with the knife, "what makes you think we want your money?"

The others laughed. "Naw," one said, "she's got a better treasure than that."

He could have, in less than a minute, killed all four of the thugs. Once he might have. But the sight of the frightened but feisty woman prevented him. While those four didn't deserve to live, neither did the woman they threatened deserve the nightmares he would leave her with if he savaged those men.

He stepped forward so they could see him. "You don't want to do that." The Voice.

They all hesitated, looking at him as if suddenly confused. The woman herself looked at him as if he were a savior. He knew better. She had no idea the kind of danger she might be in from *him*.

"Go," he said. "Go home now."

Slowly, almost like zombies, the four men turned away from the woman and began to disperse.

"Go home *now*," he repeated with more force, and they began to run.

The woman stood there, frozen, even though she should have responded to the Voice as well. Perplexing, but not the first time someone had been immune.

She was dark-haired, petite. Even with his extraordinary night vision, however, he could not see the color of her eyes. Probably too dilated from adrenaline.

"How did you do that?" she asked, barely whispering. His acute hearing picked that up, too.

"Cowards are easy to intimidate," he answered, a half-truth.

He walked toward her and she took a quick, stumbling step back. "Stay away."

He stopped. "I'm not going to leave you here alone. Where do you live?"

"I'm not telling you that!"

He almost sighed, but he could hardly blame her. "I am not leaving you here alone," he said again. He didn't want to use the Voice on her, didn't want to try it again even though it might not work. He avoided manipulating humans unless it was the only way.

"I'll get a cab."

"Where?" A faint amusement curled his thin mouth. "Don't even suggest calling one. They won't come here at night."

He saw her shoulders sag a bit. "How did you get here?" he asked, feeling his curiosity stir.

"None of your business!"

Now he *did* sigh. "I have a car. I can take you home."

"If you think I'm going to get into a car with you…"

Not even centuries of practice could give him perfect patience. He had to get this piece of bait away from the predators that lurked for blocks around, and he couldn't go back to his investigation unless he made sure she was safe. Time was passing, dawn approaching steadily and inevitably. Limited time, limited patience, now two tasks instead of one for the short hours he had.

He reached her so fast she gasped when he stood right in front of her. Then, utterly without compunction, he picked her up, hardly noticing her weight, certainly not slowed by it.

"I'm not leaving you here," he said yet again and began to stride toward his car, not as fast as he could because he didn't want to scare her any more, but fast enough.

"Let me go!"

He should have just put her to sleep. "I can take you to your home, or take you to my office, but *I am not leaving you here*."

Just a touch of the Voice. Just a hint, but it stilled her until they reached his car. So she wasn't completely impervious. Perhaps. Impossible to tell exactly what she was responding to.

He had chosen his vehicle because it wouldn't attract attention in this neighborhood: a few years too old, dented, even rusted. Not a hood ornament or hubcap to steal.

"You can't do this," she said as he put her on her feet beside the car.

"I *am* doing it. My office or your home."

"I don't want you to know where I live!"

"My office then. You'll like my assistant." He opened the passenger door for her.

Still, she hesitated. "Your assistant?"

"Chloe Crandall," he said, seeking to create a sense of normalcy for her. "A bit strange for my taste, but a nice young lady all the same. Then you can argue with *her* about how you'll get safely home."

Still stubborn, she glared at him. "Who are you?"

He reached into his breast pocket, inside his long leather coat, and passed her his business card.

Jude Messenger, Licensed Private Investigator, Messenger Investigations, Inc. Phone numbers, email, fax, but no website.

She looked up from the card at him. "A private investigator?"

"Yes." Would she ever get into the car? At this rate he'd never get back here to check into his case.

"Can I keep this?"

"Not only can you keep it, you can have a whole stack of them if you want. Leave them everywhere you go like breadcrumbs."

At that, one corner of her mouth twitched upward. Some Rubicon had been crossed in her mind. At last she slid into the car. He closed the door behind her and forced himself to walk at human speed around to the driver's side.

When he got behind the wheel, however, he gave her no further quarter. The tires squealed as he peeled away. As good as she smelled, he had to get her out of the confines of the car as quickly as possible. He couldn't afford a slip, even a minor one.

"Could you slow down, please?"

"No."

"You'll get us killed!"

He laughed. How could he not? "You're safer with me at any speed than you were back there with those guys. How did you get there?"

Silence. Well, he had more important concerns. Let her keep her secrets.

But then, hesitantly, she answered. "I was with a friend. She wanted to go to some clubs. I…ordinarily don't enjoy that, but she didn't want to go alone."

"Wise."

"Who was wise?" she asked. It almost sounded like a challenge.

"Both of you. Clubbing can be a bad scene. Going alone even worse. So let me guess. She met someone and there you were all alone."

A sigh reached him in the darkness and with it the truly enticing scent of her breath. His hands tightened on the steering wheel.

"Yes," she said presently. "She met someone, and I decided to go home. This guy she introduced me to earlier seemed safe enough. She *knew* him."

"I understand."

"So when he offered to drive me, I said yes. But he came this way, and tried to…tried to…"

He didn't need her to finish. "You ran."

"Yes."

"That's a clear picture." He wondered if he should ask her who this guy was who tried to take advantage of her, then decided she'd probably get angry at him for interfering. People rarely appreciated offers of help they hadn't asked for.

His hyperacute senses detected no heartbeats nearby at street level, at least none that weren't in the slow rhythm of sleep, so he ran a couple of red lights, certain no cops were near enough to see. He heard his passenger gasp, but he ignored it.

"Do you obey any laws?" she demanded.

"Not when they get in the way of saving lives."

"My life isn't in danger anymore."

"I'm not talking about you. I don't stroll that part of town without a reason."

"Oh."

He listened to her silence with some satisfaction. Humans tended to have such a narrow view of the world, with little real appreciation for the evils that truly existed.

A block later she asked, "I interfered?"

So she cared beyond herself. "It wasn't your fault."

"I *know* that. I'm just… I'd hate to think someone else might suffer because you saved me."

"Your danger seemed the most immediate."

"Thank you. I was terrified." And she sounded reluctant to admit it. "I'd have fought, but with four of them…" She let it trail off.

"I know." He could still smell the fear on her, though it had faded considerably. Making it easier for him to maintain control. But the scent of her blood—there was a time he would have followed that scent around the globe.

With another squeal he took a sharp corner, then zipped into a parking space in front of his office.

"We're here," he said. "I'll take you to Chloe."

It didn't look as if anything was alive or awake on the street, but one little light burned redly next to a doorbell a half dozen steps below street level. He guided her down, swiped his key in the security lock, and heard the bolt slide open.

He shoved the heavy steel door open and urged her in ahead of him. She seemed reluctant now, afraid again. Of course, the hallway was unlit out of deference to his night vision.

"Chloe?" he called out to reassure his companion.

A moment later a doorway opened in the dark hallway, and yellow light spilled forth. Chloe emerged from her office, dressed in some weird version of not-quite-punk, not-quite-stripper black leather and lace. She dyed her hair black and wore it in spikes. The whole getup was topped with an amazing amount of black eyeliner and dark shadow.

"Jude," she said, her light, youthful voice sounding surprised. "I didn't expect you for a couple of hours."

"A little hitch," he explained, motioning to the woman beside him. "She was about to be assaulted by some thugs."

Chloe, for all she was weird—and to deal with him she had to be weird—at once surged forward. "Oh, my gosh! Are you all right?"

His rescued human relaxed at last. "I'm fine, I'm fine."

"Take care of her," Jude said to Chloe. "Get her home. I've got to go back."

Chloe's eyes leapt to him even as she wrapped a supporting arm around the woman. "You mean you didn't…?"

"Not yet. I have to get back."

Chloe started to shake her head. "It's late, Jude. Way late. Let it go until tomorrow."

He'd been dealing with the threat of sunrise for nearly two hundred years. He didn't need anyone to remind him, or warn him. But when he checked internally, he reached a conclusion that displeased him.

"You're right. It'll have to wait." The passage of the night hours somehow had engraved themselves inside. Hours before dawn he could feel the sun's approach, and while he needn't fear the light until the sun fully rose, he had learned to measure his nights by an internal clock.

His clock said there wasn't enough time to retrace his steps and approach the man he'd been seeking. Not at the height of summer when the days were so long, the dawn so early.

He hated to let this matter wait. It had taken him a whole month to track down this one man. What if he moved again?

But truthfully, he would probably be able to follow the guy's trail even if he moved all the way across the city. Because he had scented it, caught it, memorized it.

Much like he'd memorized the scent of the woman he'd saved. In some corner of his brain, she was catalogued, and he could follow her anywhere. Or recognize her again even if decades or centuries passed.

Hell. He swore under his breath, watching as Chloe settled the woman with a cup of tea and plenty of youthful mothering. Himself he took into the back office, a room without windows, one where he could work even during the day if it was absolutely necessary.

It seldom was a good thing, because the sleep of death was hard to resist. And when he *did* resist it, sooner or later he had to make up for it, usually during night hours that were rightfully his.

He pulled some blood out of the refrigerator by his desk, and drained the bag without bothering to use a glass. Cold, and not completely alive, tainted with anticoagulants, it never quite satisfied the craving, but it kept him healthy. One of these days soon he needed to call on one of his acquaintances, one of those who would let him feed. No substitute quite made up for the warm, pumping blood of a living donor.

When he finished draining the bag, he sealed it away in an airtight container marked *Biohazard*. Soon the drops that were left would begin to rot, and the smell of rotting blood was even more repulsive to him than it was to humans. At all costs, that sickly odor had to be concealed.

He'd made the right decision, he told himself. By dawn that nameless woman out there would probably have been a brutalized corpse. While he couldn't read minds, he could *smell* intentions and emotions, and those thugs had been full of evil intent and a determination to leave no witness behind.

And something more. Something not quite right in their scents. Not drugs, which he could identify almost as accurately by scent as by a lab test. No, some other odor that left him feeling deeply disturbed.

He would have to deal with them eventually. Of that he had no doubt. But right now he was concerned about his more immediate target. The killer he sought was demonically oppressed, if not possessed, which meant the cops would never find him. Never. At least not until the demon was removed from the picture.

He drummed his fingers impatiently on his desk, and looked at the clock. It told him what his body already knew: not enough time, not tonight. For an ordinary killer, maybe he could squeak it in, but not a possessed one.

A knock on the door called for his attention. "Come in, Chloe." He knew it was her because her scent wafted more strongly under the door.

She pushed the door open and stuck her head in. "Our lady friend doesn't want to go home just yet, and Garner just arrived."

"Garner?" Just what he needed: a visit from an inept hunter who was trying to win his spurs while making a complete nuisance of himself. And a rescued woman who now didn't want to go home. A damn three-ring circus in his outer office.

"Sorry," Chloe whispered. "I told him you were busy but he seems to know something about the, um, target."

Things really couldn't get any better, could they? he thought sarcastically as he pushed back from his desk. Garner mixing in with a dangerous case and that woman....

Realizing he hadn't yet shucked his leather coat, he tugged it off and tossed it over his chair. It was the kind of oversight a human might notice, and he didn't want the woman to notice any more than she already had. Though he was fairly impervious to the ambient temperature, he kept the office comfortable enough for humans, like Chloe. That coat would appear out of place, and with Garner adding to the chaos of the night, he didn't want one more damn thing to seem out of place.

He stepped into the front office, his gaze first going to the woman. Not only was her scent absolutely intoxicating, but she was far prettier than he'd noticed in the earlier chaos. Long inky hair, wide blue eyes and lips that seemed to beg for a kiss. She sat in one of the client chairs near Chloe's desk, her legs crossed in a way that revealed surprising length in a woman so small. Her arms were folded tightly, but they failed to conceal the mounds of her breasts, not too small, not too large. She was as much a visual delight as an olfactory delight. Eminently desirable, eminently drinkable. A dangerous combination.

He dragged his gaze away and looked at Garner, who was leaning casually against the wall. Blond, barely twenty-four, Garner suffered from delusions of grandeur brought about by a Gift. The young man looked elegant, in a rough sort of way, and appeared composed, although Jude could smell that he was far from as calm as he appeared. "What do you want?"

"I know something about the, ah, target you're after."

"And how would you know that?"

Garner actually flushed a little. Since he wasn't undead, he still had blood pressure that responded to his emotions.

"Get in my office," Jude said impatiently. "And close the door."

Garner didn't argue, for once. He did exactly what he was told.

Then Jude returned his attention to beautiful and problematic woman. "Why don't you want to go home?"

She bit her lower lip, revealing a glimpse of perfect, white teeth. "Because that guy who offered me a ride? He knows where I live."

Chloe spread her hands as if to say, *How can you argue with that?*

Easy. "Chloe will take you to the police.

File a complaint against him for sexual assault. They'll run him down."

"But I don't have any proof he did anything. And if I go to the police…" Again she stopped, as if unwilling to say more. "I don't want to make him madder," she said finally.

"More likely he'll cool down and decide he made a big mistake. Maybe he just had too much to drink."

The woman shook her head, biting her lip harder.

Jude smothered a sigh. "What aren't you telling me?"

The woman hesitated, then the words came out of her in a rush. "I kicked him in the groin. And he got so mad he started to swing at me and that's when I stabbed him."

"Stabbed him?" Had Jude been mortal he was sure that by this point he'd be looking for a double whiskey and a chair.

"With a pen," she said quickly. "It's not like I had a knife or anything."

Jude decided on the chair after all. And maybe a whiskey later, though it would have little effect on him. He sat.

Rachel Lee 27

"How badly did you stab him?"

"Not too badly. I got him in the shoulder and I'm pretty sure the pen couldn't have gone in more than two inches, max. I'm fairly certain I didn't hit anything but muscle. Then I got out of the car and started running, and he chased me for maybe half a block screaming he was going to kill me."

"Oh." He wondered how he had missed that part of the night's activity. Probably too focused on what he was there to do, or maybe he'd arrived shortly after this altercation. Either way… So the guy had threatened to kill her. Even on his most sanguine day he couldn't dismiss such a threat out of hand.

He looked at Chloe, then looked at the woman. "What's your name?"

"Terri. Theresa Black."

"Okay, Theresa Black, are you absolutely certain you're telling me the truth?"

"Why wouldn't I?"

"Because there could have been other reasons to stab this guy."

He smelled the indignation as much as he

saw it. All right, she was telling the truth. She'd defended herself from an attacker.

Chloe spoke. "You don't have time."

"You're always worried about my time," he grumped at her.

"Maybe because I don't want to look for another job? You don't have time tonight. There's Garner. And other things."

Like he needed her to remind him.

"Don't have time for what?" Theresa asked.

"Never mind," he answered shortly. His inner clock was starting to tick more loudly, warning of dawn's approach. He glanced at the clock on Chloe's desk and saw he had less than two hours. Not enough to hunt down a man he knew nothing about.

He looked at Chloe. "I want all the information on the guy who attacked her. Every detail. Right away."

"Yes, boss."

"Then you and I are taking her to the cops."

"Maybe Garner could…"

He interrupted her with a look. "Garner? You've got to be kidding."

"Well, it was a thought. He's got to learn sometime."

"Not today. Garner can turn the smallest task into an earth-shattering catastrophe. I don't have time to clean up after him. No Garner."

"I don't want to go to the cops," Theresa said firmly. "That'll just make things worse with Sam. And if they keep me too long, I'll be late to work. I can't afford that."

"Call in sick." Jude had had enough. Another minute in the same room with this woman and he might revert. He rose. "If you don't go to the police, if you go home or go to work instead, then I take no responsibility for anything that happens to you."

Turning, he walked into his office. Before he closed the door he heard Theresa say, "Is he always so harsh?"

"Only when his night gets messed up."

Then he closed the door, leaving the problem of Theresa in the capable hands of Chloe, so he could face the much less capable hands of Garner.

Garner lounged in the client chair facing

Jude's desk, one leg thrown over the arm. The instant Jude entered, however, he straightened up, putting both feet on the floor.

Jude said nothing as he rounded the desk and took his own seat. Only then did he speak. "What the hell are you doing here, Garner?"

The younger man shrugged. "I smelled the, ah, target."

"And?"

"I smelled that same odor somewhere else, earlier today. On someone else."

At that Jude straightened a bit. "Victim?"

Garner shook his head. He might still be new at all this, but he was sure of his innate instincts. "The oppression involves more than the one guy you found."

"Hell."

Garner leaned forward, a little too eagerly. "Look, I know you think I'm too untrained to help at all. I still haven't figured out how you think I'm going to *get* trained if you keep me out of all the action. But even *you* know how good my gift is. And I'm telling you, this is no minor infestation. I bet if I keep moving around town, I'll find others."

It was possible, entirely too possible. Such things had happened before, and when they did they invariably signaled a huge problem right around the corner.

"We need to stop it before there are five of them," Garner said. As if Jude didn't already know. He reached into his pocket and pulled out a scrap of paper. "I followed the guy home. We can find him here."

Jude caved, just a little. Reaching into his desk he pulled out a container of pushpins. "Put it on the map." The map of the city that was tacked to one wall. The red pin already there indicated the target he'd been after tonight.

Garner seemed pleased to be allowed to do even this much. Jude, remembering other times when Garner's attempts to help had proved more problematic than anything, wondered once again what he was going to do with this young man before the kid got himself into serious trouble. The dead kind of trouble.

Garner marked the spot with a blue pin and returned to his seat. "I can help," he said again.

Jude leaned forward resting on his elbows. "Here's how it's going to be, Garner."

The kid's face brightened hopefully.

"You're going to do a sweep. Start at dawn. Cover as much of the city as you can and report back here at sunset. I need to know how many cases we have."

Garner nodded. "Absolutely."

"The more there are of them, the faster I need to work. Clear? And you're not going to get in the way, and you're not going to do anything stupid. You're just going to report back."

Garner's hope appeared to be tempered with a touch of disappointment, but he nodded again. "I can do that."

Jude tapped the desk with a fingertip to emphasize his point. "You are not ready to deal with these guys. Are we clear on that? If they catch on to you, you run the risk of infestation or possession yourself. So you're going to prove to me that you know how to be very cautious, understood?"

"And if I do?"

Jude sighed, knowing there was no way out of this. If the infestation was spreading, he might not be able to keep up without help from someone who could hunt during daylight hours. "If you prove that you can follow orders exactly, I'll think about the next step in your training."

"Thanks, Jude!" Garner leapt up, having won at last. Or so he thought.

Jude knew better. Garner had no idea of the realities of the world he was trying to enter. No idea at all.

But when Garner opened the door of Jude's office, the scent of Theresa Black wafted in. God. Jude almost banged his head on his desk. A screwed-up night, and now the most enticing morsel he'd encountered in at least fifty years was out there in his extra room, close enough to…

No.

He forced himself to look at the wall map, but two pins did not a pattern make, and he knew he was fooling himself, thinking he could gain a thing by pondering two locations.

Sometimes he hated his belated development of a conscience. Sometimes he hated his self-imposed exile.

It was several centuries too late to start thinking that he could use a hobby of some kind to fill hours.

Damn, he hated it when a night got messed up.

A couple of minutes later, Jude stood just inside his office, the door ajar, listening. He knew he was being a damn fool, maybe a double-damned fool, but that woman's scent kept drawing him.

"Your boss is a strange man."

Jude smelled Chloe bristle, heard it in her voice. Despite all the instincts that were urging him to walk in there and take what he wanted, he had to smile faintly. Chloe couldn't have been more protective of him if she'd been his own mother. In fact, come to think of it, his own mother hadn't cared that much.

Chloe said, "That's a nice thing to say about a guy who just saved your life."

"I didn't mean it that way. Just that he's… different."

"We're all different in some way. Jude gets pretty intense when he's working a tough case."

"Okay." Theresa sighed. "Sorry. But Jude is a little, well, overwhelming. It was kind of weird the way he made those guys leave. And then he moved so fast!"

Chloe responded easily, even as her fingers typed rapidly at the keyboard, no doubt researching Terri's assailant. "He's a sprinter. Or was."

Good lie, Chloe. Sometimes he thought Chloe would lie under oath to protect him. He hoped they never had to find out.

"I guess that would explain it."

"You need to talk?"

"I'm just trying to absorb it all." Theresa laughed uneasily. "I moved from one near rape to another in a matter of a few minutes, then your avenger boss came out of nowhere and cowed those guys as if…as if by magic."

"It's his confidence," Chloe said. "Most cowards won't take on a man who knows he can take them out."

"Really? There were four of them." And she sounded awfully dubious. He couldn't blame her.

"And Jude knows all the martial arts. He'd

have had them all flat on their faces before you could blink."

"Oh." Theresa didn't sound as if she quite believed it.

Well, not *all* the martial arts, Jude thought, mildly amused. His inhuman speed had a lot to do with it.

"Look," Chloe said after a minute, "you don't have to worry about Jude. I've worked with him for four years now, and I can promise you he's one of the good guys."

"That's good to know."

"Yeah, he has his moods. He can get impatient. He hates it when his night gets messed up. He even gets crabby and short-tempered at times. You know, like the rest of us."

At that Theresa gave a small laugh. "Okay. It's just... I'm sorry. He's your boss and you like him."

"Just what?"

"Well, somehow he *feels* different. I can't explain it."

"He *is* different," Chloe said. "If this were a comic book, he'd probably be one of the superheroes."

He really needed to tell Chloe not to go over the top like that. That was downright embarrassing.

Theresa spoke again. "What's he going to do with the information about the guy who tried to attack me in his car?"

"Well, if the cops don't have enough to arrest him, I suspect Jude will pay him a visit and convince him to forget he ever met you."

Too close to the truth, Chloe. Watch it.

"How is that going to help? It'll probably just make the guy madder."

"Trust me," Chloe said, "when Jude puts the fear of God into someone, it sticks."

Terri asked for the restroom and Chloe offered to show the way.

Jude had fully opened the door of his office when Chloe emerged from the hallway to the restroom. She saw him and glared at him, obviously annoyed that he'd been eavesdropping.

Not that he cared. He jerked his head toward his office, then went inside to wait. And Chloe, of course, made him wait. She must have filled the teakettle and put it on the stove before she meandered his way. Chloe drank tea as if it were the staff of life.

"Close the door," he said.

"Eavesdroppers rarely hear anything good." She sniffed as she closed the door.

"I'm glad I listened. You need to avoid making me sound like Superman."

Chloe shrugged. "I gotta explain it somehow, boss. You keep doing these little things that make people suspicious."

"Only when I have no choice."

"Choice or not, that woman is observant. Scared as she was, she noticed things. So how do you want me to explain it? Oh, my boss is a vampire?"

He glared at her.

She glared back.

"Just watch it," he said finally.

"If you watch it better, I can watch it better." Chloe sniffed yet again, evincing worlds of disapproval. "You ought to be grateful I'm such an inventive liar."

With that she pointed at the clock wordlessly, then walked out.

Jude stared at the closed door, and finally

gave in to a grin. It was too damn bad Chloe wasn't his type.

Then, gauging his time, he decided he could at least escort Terri and Chloe to the nearest precinct station and get the process rolling before he'd need to hurry back here.

More time with that woman and her narcotic scent. He needed to have his head examined.

Chapter 2

An hour before dawn, even police stations experienced a lull. While hospitals were in their most critical hours, the rest of the city, including the criminal element, was finally sinking into sleep.

Well, it was a relative lull, anyway. Jude accompanied Theresa, who looked singularly unhappy, and Chloe, who looked as if she were enjoying this change of pace, into the station and up to the desk sergeant. As a PI, he wasn't entirely unknown in some of the precincts, though seldom was his arrival truly welcome.

Sgt. Davies knew him, though, and greeted

him pleasantly enough, though not exactly warmly.

"Ms. Black," Jude explained, "needs to file a report. She was attacked twice tonight down near Mason and Crick, and I witnessed the second attack."

Davies's eyes leapt to Terri as Jude indicated her with a wave of his hand. "Twice? Crap." Then he looked at Jude. "And I suppose you're in your usual rush?"

Jude frowned at him. "All I can do is confirm part of her story. And I do have an urgent case."

"You always have an urgent case." Davies sighed. "Well, you're in luck. I'll get you to Detective Matthews. She always seems to have time for you."

Not entirely the detective's own choice, thought Jude with grim satisfaction. He'd implanted a suggestion four years ago, and occasionally reinforced it. And he certainly found it useful to have an ally of sorts within the police.

In less than five minutes they were in the Robbery-Homicide squad room, although the case would probably be better handled by the sex crimes unit. Regardless, Matthews never refused to see Jude.

She was a tall woman of about forty with a no-nonsense air and short gray-flecked hair. Attractive, but in a subdued way. She chose not to flaunt.

The squad room was even more quiet than the rest of the station because those on shift were out on cases that had occurred tonight, and the rest were doing what mortals do at that hour: sleeping at home.

"Okay," Matthews asked. "What happened?"

Once again Terri seemed reluctant, so Jude plunged into describing what he knew, and giving a description of the four thugs who had surrounded her. And he was starting to get impatient because the prickling on the back of his neck had begun to grow uncomfortable. He glanced at the large wall clock across the room. Forty-five minutes and he had to be home. Period.

Matthews took Terri's personal information, then asked her, "What do you do for a living?"

"I'm a forensic pathologist. I just started working at the M.E.'s office last week. And, Detective, I can't be late for my shift."

A forensic pathologist? Hot damn, Jude thought. A contact of that kind could be extremely useful.

Matthews smiled at Terri. "I'll be as quick as I can, but I think the M.E. would be understanding if you're a little late because you're a material witness."

"Maybe. I'm so new, though."

Pat Matthews's eyes softened. "Honey, I know it's awful. All of it. But you've got to help us get these cruds off the street. You wouldn't want to be responsible for it happening to someone else, would you?"

Terri shook her head and straightened her shoulders. "No, of course not. Except I don't have any evidence to offer. Other than that I stabbed Sam with a pen. I can't prove he attacked me. Or that those other guys wanted to."

"I understand. We may not be able to do anything immediately, but having your statement on file could help us in the future."

Terri nodded. "All right then."

Jude stood and started pacing. Night was drawing to a close, and being this far away from his lair at this time always made him uncomfortable, even when he knew for a fact that he could make it back in time.

Finally as the minutes ticked by, with Terri telling her story in detail and Chloe offering the information she had gathered on the Sam guy, he could take it no longer. It wasn't as if he absolutely had to be here, a situation which would help him overcome his growing discomfort. No, he was basically a fifth wheel, and he'd already told Matthews everything he knew.

"I've got to go. If you need me to sign anything or answer any more questions, I can come back tonight."

The detective hesitated only a moment. "All right. I'll let Chloe know if I need more."

"Thanks. Good night. Oh, Chloe? I'll leave you the car." He tossed her the keys and strode out.

Twenty minutes later, back at his office, he locked his own office door, three dead bolts and a key-code entry. But his bedroom was something else. Getting it built without arousing interest or suspicion or creating talk had been quite an achievement.

It was basically an oversize vault, with a time lock that would not open until after sunset unless he opened it from the inside. The room itself had been decorated to look like an ordinary bedroom, in case someone happened on it when it was unlocked. But since he was nearly defenseless in the sleep of death, the price of this kind of protection hadn't mattered. Not since the night forty years ago when he had been discovered in sleep by accident and had awakened in a morgue with a tag around his toe.

Once he was locked in his vault, however, the building could burn down around him, a bomb could fall, and nobody would get in. At least not before he woke up and was ready to emerge, in charge of himself and the situation.

Quite an improvement over a few hundred years ago.

He had even managed to make it a little

homey, while revealing nothing about himself. Not that he spent much waking time in here.

It was, really, a crypt and he knew it. Occasionally, he fantasized about being able to share it with someone, but he knew that would never happen. He'd never turn anyone into what he was, and no human could ever endure this life for long.

Not even Chloe, who had, for a while, had a crush on him. He'd saved her, too, one dark night, and like a puppy she had followed him home. And she had noticed enough during that awful scene to figure out what he was.

Amazing. Most humans wouldn't believe it even when they saw it, not these days. They always thought it must be some gag. Or that they were imagining things, because everyone knew vampires were myth.

Except Chloe, and a few others he trusted just enough. And most of those others…well, he would bet most thought he was just a member of a vampire cult, the way they were. He doubted many of them thought he was the real thing.

He felt the sun's rising, though he could not

see it. It prickled along the back of his neck, and told him it was time. He stripped quickly and slipped between silk sheets. Not because he would be aware of anything between now and sunset, but because when he awoke he wanted to be comfortable.

His head hit the pillow. The prickling strengthened. And then with a sigh, he died.

"God, he's weird," Matthews said after Jude departed. "He always tears out of here like he has a rocket on his tail, especially in the early morning."

"He can't help it," Chloe said. "He's got a disease."

Matthews arched her brows. "What disease?"

"I can't remember what it's called. He can't get into bright light, especially sunlight. Blisters, burns…why can't I ever remember what it's called?"

"Oh, come on," Matthews said.

"No," Terri offered. "It's called xeroderma pigmentosum. Rare but real." She looked at

Chloe. "That's awful. I can't imagine living with that."

Chloe gave a little shrug. "He seems to have adapted pretty well."

Matthews still looked doubtful. "That's a real disease? How fast can he burn?"

"Probably with just a few seconds of exposure he'd have the kind of sunburn that would put most people in the hospital," Terri said. "Most people with it don't survive long, because even fluorescent lighting can cause burns in some cases. Given how little people know about the disease, it's a miracle he's still alive."

"Well, that would explain why he's so pale," Matthews commented. "Imagine never seeing the sun. So you learned about it in medical school?"

"Actually," Terri said, "I learned about it during an investigation when I was a pathology resident. We had a case the police thought for sure was murder, the kid was so severely burned. The first assumption was that one of his parents must have literally boiled him alive. But there was no evidence of assault, nor were the burns anywhere near as severe where his clothes were thick, like his diaper."

"Oh, ugh," said Chloe.

"But the pathologist I was training with did some genetic testing, when the parents insisted all they had done was take the baby to a lakeside picnic. Anyway, he found the markers."

"And it killed the kid?" Matthews sounded amazed.

"Every bit of exposed skin was blistered. The most exposed areas even exhibited third-degree burns. Most people have milder cases than that baby, but yes, when you've got an extreme case, even a tiny bit of sun can kill you."

"Live and learn." Matthews shook her head. "Okay, to get back to your case. I doubt we can arrest Sam Carlisle for anything, unless you have some kind of injury yourself?"

Terri shook her head. "It all happened so fast. Honestly. If I have any bruises, I'll find out during the day. He did grab my arm awfully tight, but I don't bruise easily."

Matthews nodded sympathetically. "I'll do a background on him and see if anyone else has ever had trouble with him. But without some physical evidence, it'll be hard."

"I know. Jude just thought I should report it."

"He's right. You should, and you did. I'll type up your statement and you can sign it later, okay? In the meantime you probably need to go home, shower, sleep a little and get ready for your shift."

Terri managed a smile. "Thank you, Detective."

Pat Matthews shrugged. "Look at it this way—if the creep comes in to file a complaint against you for stabbing him with that pen, you're covered. We won't listen very hard."

"I didn't even think of that."

"And as for those other creeps Jude scared off, well, if they try it on someone else, your statement will back the victim up. Can you come back after your shift to look at some mug shots?"

"Sure. It was dark, though."

"You never know. You might recognize someone. It's worth a shot." She looked at

Chloe. "And tell that boss of yours I want him to look at the mug shots, too."

"I will," Chloe answered as she stood. Then she turned to Terri. "Come by the office tomorrow when you get off work, and I'll bring you back to look at those mug shots. Now let me drive you home. You're not the only one who needs a shower and bed. It's been a long night."

Not even a cup of herbal tea helped Terri relax into sleep. Too much had happened in the hours just past, and her mind and emotions struggled to cope with them. Attempted rape, not once but twice. She'd stabbed a man. Every time she remembered that, the way it had felt, the realization of what she had done, she shuddered again.

Nor did it help that she had to get to work around ten. The idea of only a couple of hours of sleep seemed to make it harder yet to close her eyes.

And then there was Jude Messenger, private investigator. Eyes as dark as the night he had emerged from, turning an odd shade of dark gold when he stepped into the light. A man only slightly taller than average, but somehow seeming much, much larger. That voice of his when he'd told those men to go. If she hadn't been paralyzed with fright, she probably would have obeyed that order herself.

The incredible speed with which he had approached her, so fast it had almost seemed he was there picking her up before she had seen him move. But of course that was impossible. Absolutely impossible. Her recollections must be marred by the fear that had been raging in her. The adrenaline.

The man had rescued her, yet he had left her feeling supremely uneasy, anyway. And she couldn't really understand why. His office was normal enough. His assistant Chloe was perfectly normal. Even Garner, that handsome young man, had seemed typical, even though she got the impression Jude considered him to be some kind of plague.

So what was it about Jude Messenger?

She lay on her side, keeping the locked door in sight, making sure that even if she shut her eyes, they would open trained on the only place from which a threat could come.

Somehow she couldn't feel safe. Was she really worried that Sam might carry out his threat to kill her? Or was it just a holdover from the earlier hours? She didn't even want to turn off the small lamp by the bed, although sunlight had long since begun peeking around the edges of the curtained window above the bed.

And the feeling she had right now reminded her all too much of her childhood, when fear had kept her awake countless nights, fear of something she could not see, could only sense and finally, to her horror, hear. The haunting. But this was different. Surely?

Yet, in some way she felt as if she had brushed up against that evil again during the past night.

A shudder passed through her, and she forced herself to breathe deeply and slowly, calming herself. That evil had been gone from her life for sixteen years now. There was absolutely no reason to think she'd ever encounter it again.

But her thoughts refused to be entirely corralled and kept returning to Jude. He, too, made her uneasy. He might be a little...different, but he had saved her from those beasts, and had brought her to a safe place where Chloe had become an instant friend. Then he had even gone so far as to accompany her to the police.

So what was it about him? She had to admit that along with the uneasiness he made her feel, she also found him undeniably attractive. Maybe thirty, she thought. Maybe a bit older. Something in his eyes, when they turned golden, made her think he was older.

He was definitely handsome. No, not exactly that. Good-looking, yes, but he was even more attractive in another way. Something visceral in her responded to him. Maybe that was what made her so uneasy.

It had been a long time, a decade or more, since simply seeing a man had been enough to make her aware of fluttery, eager femininity. Of desire. And she'd been aware of it every single second in his presence, despite everything that had been happening.

Pretty amazing, actually, but pretty unnerving, too. Even his gruffness and impatience hadn't put an end to it.

She closed her eyes and gave up, hugging the unexpected, nearly forgotten feeling somewhere deep inside. No one would ever know, and it was nice to realize she could still feel that way. At twenty-nine, she had thought she would no longer feel those things. Too many other things, adult things, kept getting in the way.

But somehow the mere sight of Jude Messenger had swept away the layers of the years and made her young enough in some way to just respond to man's appearance and voice, and get a thrill from it.

Kind of neat, actually, now that she had figured it out.

Satisfied she had identified the source of at least part of her uneasiness, she curled more comfortably on the bed and finally let sleep crawl closer.

Surely her uneasiness had nothing to do with that haunting when she was a child, no matter how it felt. How could it? It had been so long ago.

No, of course that had nothing to do with it. She was just feeling uneasy because it had been so long since she'd felt such a powerful attraction. She didn't want that now, didn't have time for it.

All in all, though, it had been one heck of a night. And at last her eyes fluttered closed.

The Medical Examiner, Steve Crepo, sent Terri home a little early when he heard the reason for her obvious fatigue. Her usual shift ran from ten to eight four days a week, with a brief lunch break. "You should have just called in and explained," he told her.

"I'm the newbie. Besides, honestly, I didn't want to spend all day thinking about last night."

He nodded understandingly over his half-rimmed eyeglasses. A little plump and balding, he had a kindly face which belied the strict way he ran the M.E.'s office. He did have the somewhat disconcerting habit of treating the cadavers as if they might still be alive, and referring to them by name rather than number. It was almost as if he saw himself running a surgical suite rather than a morgue.

In one way Terri liked that about him. In another she found it discomfiting, because his idiosyncrasy had already begun to chip away that carefully trained distance she had been taught to place between herself and the dead. She found herself on guard, for fear she might lose objectivity.

Although there were inevitably cases where objectivity went out the window, terrible cases, mostly those involving small children. Then anger and horror often overrode all self-protective mechanisms.

"I understand," he told her now. "But remember, if you're overtired, you can make mistakes. We can't have that."

"No, sir."

He smiled. "So go home and rest up. I'll see you tomorrow morning."

She showered and changed back into street clothes before leaving, washing the smell of death out of her very pores. That odor clung and sometimes she wasn't sure that even three shampooings got it all out of her hair.

Outside the sun hadn't quite yet set, and that for some reason made her think of Jude Messenger. A man confined to the hours of darkness, who had nevertheless managed to cobble together a useful life, and even, apparently, some very loyal friends, to judge by Chloe.

Remembering Chloe's promise to accompany her to look at mug shots, and feeling an oddly strong compulsion to follow through even though she was exhausted, she got off the bus near Jude's office and rang the bell.

Chloe's voice greeted her. "Messenger Investigations."

"Hi, Chloe, it's Terri Black."

"Hey, Terri. Come on in."

She walked down the now-familiar dark hallway as Chloe opened the door and leaned out.

"How are you doing?" Chloe asked.

"I'm tired but fine. I guess we should go to the precinct and look at mug shots, but I can barely see straight."

Chloe laughed, inviting her in, then closing the door behind them. "I slept most of the day," she volunteered. "Jude's not going with us. Says he'll get to it later. Did you want to see him, too?"

Terri hesitated. "I guess. I never really thanked him."

"He's not real big on the gratitude thing. Sort of like the Lone Ranger, you know? 'Who was that masked man?'"

Terri laughed. "You make him sound like a superhero."

Chloe started to giggle again, but at that moment her eyes widened a shade. "Hi, Jude. Sleep well?"

Theresa turned to find Jude Messenger standing in the doorway of his office, a study in chiaroscuro, all black and white from his hair to his boots. His eyes were dark again, and she realized the last of the daylight had vanished, leaving only the low light of a couple of small lamps. Her heart thumped, and she felt that magnetic pull once more. How could she have forgotten how good a man could look? Especially in black slacks and a very nicely tailored black shirt.

"Like the dead," he answered, sounding almost sarcastic. "Didn't I tell you to stop trying to turn me into Superman?"

Chloe sniffed. "I'm just saying I like the kinds of things you do. They make me feel good about our business."

He gave a little shake of his head, as if he knew he wasn't going to win this argument with Chloe. "Did Garner show up?"

"Not yet. Was he supposed to?"

"Around sunset."

"Well, he's not that late then."

Jude crossed the room, pulled a wooden chair away from the wall and straddled it, facing the two women from a few feet away. He folded his arms across its back. "I need to take care of that guy so Dr. Black here doesn't have to worry about him. And I have that other case. I was hoping Garner would show up first."

"He'll probably be here any minute. Why? Is he working for us now? You usually groan when you hear his name."

"I may groan again before too long."

Those dark eyes settled on Theresa, and she

felt her skin prickle. Awareness? Or something else? She couldn't tell.

"How are you feeling, Dr. Black?"

"Just call me Terri. I'm fine, thank you. And I doubt you need to do anything about Sam." Although she had to admit she wasn't one hundred percent sure of that, given that she had stabbed him. He might well be the kind to want to get even. How would she know? She'd certainly looked at enough women on the autopsy table who had misjudged a man's thirst for vengeance.

"Yes, I do." His tone brooked no argument. "What's his full name again?"

"Samuel Carlisle," Chloe answered promptly. She pulled out a drawer in her desk and retrieved a file. "Everything I could find on him from what Terri told me."

Theresa was amazed. She hadn't expected Chloe to go to all that trouble. After all, even the police had only wanted the basics.

But Jude opened the file and began reading, and apparently it was more than just name and address. "Hmm," he said finally.

"Hmm?" Theresa asked.

Those dark eyes lifted to her again. Hunter's eyes, she thought, wondering why she almost felt like a mouse staring down a hawk.

"Hmm," he repeated.

"That means 'not good,'" Chloe interpreted. "Not good how?"

Jude tossed the file and it landed on Chloe's desk. "I'm going to have a very interesting talk with Samuel Carlisle."

"Why?" Her heart fluttered a little, because she didn't like the dark tone in his voice.

"Because he needs one."

Theresa looked at Chloe, begging with her eyes for an explanation.

Chloe glanced at Jude. Jude shrugged, as if he didn't care. Chloe turned back to her. "Because your friend Sam has been investigated for date rape before. He's on the street only because the woman withdrew her complaint."

"Oh, my God!" Terri's hand clapped to her mouth, and for an instant she wondered if the remains of her lunch were going to come up. "Oh, my God."

"God has nothing to do with it," Jude said grimly. His eyes seemed to have grown even darker. He pushed himself out of the chair and looked down at Theresa. "You were lucky. Last time the woman claimed he used Rohypnol."

The date rape drug. Theresa sat frozen, her stomach churning, remembering last night. He'd bought her a drink. A drink she hadn't wanted. One he kept insisting she enjoy until finally, when he was distracted, she'd dumped most of it on the floor behind her chair. "Oh, God," she whispered. "I didn't drink it. I dumped it."

Chloe jumped up from her chair and came around her desk to put a hand on Theresa's shoulder. "Jude will take care of him. He'll never dare come near you again."

"But…the cops will find out the same thing you did. Won't they take care of it?"

Chloe answered, "Not the way Jude will."

The words hardly registered, because another feeling washed over her, one of sheer fury. "I wish I'd stabbed that pen into his heart!"

Surprisingly, a laugh issued from Jude. She looked at him, unable to understand what was so funny. "I mean it!"

"I know." The brief laugh disappeared from his face. "Hell." He sighed.

"Jude," Chloe said warningly.

He glared at her, an expression that Terri was sure would have made *her* sink to the floor in a quivering puddle. The man looked capable of murder.

"I'll deal with him."

"But how?" Terri demanded. "How can you?"

His dark gaze returned to her, nearly pinning her. "First," he said slowly, very quietly, "I am going to ensure he never so much as *thinks* about coming near you again. Unlike the police, I can use threats. Okay?"

Terri managed a jerky nod.

Jude's attention returned to Chloe. "She doesn't leave here until I get back or call and say it's okay. Got it?"

Chloe nodded. "You can count on me."

"And if Master Garner ever drags his behind in here, nail his feet to the floor until I say otherwise. I mean it, Chloe. Don't let him go running out. I swear that kid has a death wish."

On that grumpy statement, Jude disappeared

into his office only to return a moment later wearing his long leather coat.

He paused just long enough to pick up Sam's photo, then look at Terri and say, "Stay. I mean it. This guy is bigger trouble than I originally suspected."

She didn't think she could have moved to save her life.

And only when he left the room did she feel she could breathe again.

Once he was in his battered car, Jude took a moment to clear his head, nose and lungs of Terri's scent. God in heaven, that woman's scent was like a drug. Being in the same room with her was enough to drive him nuts. In no time flat she pushed him to the edges of self-control in a way he hadn't experienced in at least fifty or so years.

The Hunger raged in him, but that alone wouldn't have put him so much on edge. No, it was the desire he felt for her, pounding and strong, stronger than any he had ever felt as a man, stronger than any he had ever felt as an immortal. The feeling was so powerful that it could have turned him into the kind of creep he was about to go see.

Breathing deeply, he battered the insanity back into the buried, darkest places of his being. The places he had vowed never to visit again.

Madness was no longer welcome in his world.

But certain forms of vengeance were.

Chapter 3

As Jude had suspected, Samuel Carlisle was in no mood to paint the town that night, not after having been stabbed just the night before. Whether or not he had been visited by the cops, and Jude strongly suspected he hadn't, he undoubtedly thought by now that he was safe. Little did he know.

So there he was, opening his own door, looking sour and saying before Jude could speak, "I don't want any."

"You're going to get it, anyway," Jude replied, his smile glacial. With a shove, one that required very little effort for him, he pushed the door hard enough to make it slam all the way open. At once Sam started backing up. Fear entered his gaze. "I'll call the cops, man. You better get out."

Jude's smile widened. "No, you won't call anyone." The Voice.

It froze Sam in his tracks as Jude entered the apartment and closed the door. "We need to have a talk."

"About what?" Sam's defiance was rising again, and he started edging toward a phone on the coffee table.

"Stop."

Sam froze again. Jude closed the distance between them, caught Sam under his chin with one hand and lifted him off the floor. Sam stared wildly at him, but didn't try to fight.

"Look into my eyes," Jude ordered.

Sam obeyed, not really having any choice at the moment. Jude shoved him up against a wall so he wouldn't strangle the guy. Although he was tempted. So very tempted.

"Listen to me."

Sam stared in hypnotic horror.

"You will not *ever* go anywhere near Theresa Black again. Do I make myself clear?"

A small nod.

"You will not ever attempt to rape another woman."

"No." A squeak.

"Because if you ever again attempt to use Rohypnol on anyone, if you ever again attempt to take a woman without her express and freely given permission, I will hunt you to the ends of the earth and rip out your throat. Are we clear?"

"Yeah."

"In fact, let me take this one step further. If you ever, *ever* even so much as *think* of using Rohypnol or force again, you are going to walk yourself to the nearest police station and turn yourself in. Got it?"

"Yeah."

"Failing that, you're going to jump off the highest building you can find. Because if I have to come after you, you will wish you had never been born. Understood?"

A croaky *yes* answered him.

Jude held the man's gaze, making sure

the suggestions had taken solid root. Then for good measure he added, "You will forget Theresa Black. You never met her. You never talked to her. You never knew her and you will head the other way if you ever see her."

"I...don't...know her."

Jude let go and watched the man collapse to the floor. Then he squatted and lifted Sam's chin with one finger until the man had to look at him again.

"I am your worst nightmare," Jude said. "Forget last night. Remember my directions."

"Yesss..."

"Remember me."

Sam's eyes closed.

Satisfied, Jude stood and walked out of the apartment, closing the door behind him.

Well, not one hundred percent satisfied. He would have cheerfully drained the guy dry, to ensure he would never threaten anyone again, but in these days of modern forensics and advanced detection, he couldn't leave a blood trail behind him. Ever.

And he was fairly certain his suggestions about never doing this again would wear off eventually. Yes, the guy would avoid Theresa, because she was specific. But the more general threat, well, his compulsions would eventually start to win out against it.

And eventually Jude would have to come for him again.

In some ways, life had been easier a century or two ago. In others, less so. Frankly, sometimes he wasn't sure which was better.

But one thing was constant, and that was evil. True evil.

Outside, after he was in his car, he flipped open his phone and called Chloe. She answered on the first ring, knowing it was him because she insisted on having caller ID.

"Hi," she said. And for once she didn't sound cheerful.

His instincts kicked into high gear, but first things first. "Tell Terri it's safe to go home. Did Garner get there?"

"Uh…boss?"

"What?"

"I think you'd better come back."

"I have another job, remember?"

"I think," Chloe repeated evenly, "that you'd better get back here now."

"Is anyone bleeding?"

"Not yet. But Garner may be soon."

"What did he do?"

"Jude," she said, this time almost shrieking, "just get back here now!"

That did it. His tires barely hit the pavement on the way back.

He burst into his business suite to find Chloe standing in front of the closed door of his inner office and Garner trying to vanish into the far corner.

"I just went to the bathroom," Chloe said at the same time Garner protested, "I thought she knew!"

And in an instant, he guessed what had happened. "Where's Terri?"

"Locked in your office," Chloe said, staring daggers at Garner. "That damn fool told her. *Told* her!"

"I thought she knew!"

Jude shook his head as if to loosen something. Astonishment nearly overwhelmed him. "She believed it?"

"She not only believed it, she locked herself in your office. I had to cut the phones off in there."

He reflected for a bare instant that he was glad he'd insisted on that feature so he couldn't be disturbed when he wanted total privacy.

"She's threatening to call the cops," Chloe said.

"They won't believe her."

"Who cares?" Chloe threw up her hand. "Who cares if *they* believe her. *She* believes it, she won't come out, she's terrified and hysterical and who knows what she'll find in your desk or… Tell me you locked the fridge."

She was almost pleading.

"I put all that stuff in my bedroom. It's locked."

A puff of breath escaped Chloe and she sagged. "Thank goodness." Then she turned on Garner. "I swear I'm going to cut you into little pieces and feed you to my fish, you idiot!"

Garner's eyes were huge. "I'll tell her I was making it up."

"She's obviously not going to believe that

now, you turkey! She saw some things last night. I had it all explained, and then you, *you...*"

"Calm down," Jude said. "Just calm the hell down and let me think."

He knew he could get into his office, locked or not. He had the code, after all, and the key card. But he wasn't sure that would be wise, at least not yet.

He looked at Chloe again. "She really believed it?"

"Well, I don't think she locked herself in your office because she thought Garner was telling a tall tale. And she certainly didn't try to call the cops because she thought she was hearing the new and updated version of *Grimm's Fairy Tales.*"

Garner dared to clear his throat. "You can make her forget."

Jude merely looked at him. "She didn't exactly respond to the Voice last night."

"Oh."

No, when he'd told those guys to leave, there was no reason Terri shouldn't have attempted to follow the order. He'd expected to have to go after her. Instead she had just stood there. Which meant… Well, it might well mean he couldn't vamp her at all. He didn't know, and frankly he didn't want to try. It was a kind of violation he preferred not to inflict on innocent people.

However… He sighed and sat beside Chloe's desk, drumming his fingers and looking at Garner. The young man seemed to shrink.

"I have to get in there by dawn," he remarked.

Garner nodded violently, as if by emphasizing his agreement he could salvage something.

"And then there's the job I'm not getting done."

Garner gulped.

"And of course the matter of a needlessly terrified woman."

Chloe spoke. "Like I said, he's an *idiot!*"

Jude frowned at her. Not that he disagreed, it was just that such statements were pointless. That was one of the things he'd managed to learn in over two hundred years.

Although occasionally he indulged in them himself.

"Garner?"

"Yes, sir?"

Oh, now he was *sir*. "You give me a headache. I haven't had a headache since I died, but you've managed to give me a headache."

"Sorry."

Chloe glared at Garner. "Fish food," she said.

"I thought she knew."

Chloe folded her arms. "Blabbing confidential information just because you *think* someone knows makes you untrustworthy, you dweeb. And you want to work with us? Hah!"

"I'll find a way to make it up, I swear."

"Too little too late, you dummy."

"Enough," Jude said. "Grinding him under your heel isn't going to fix this."

"I'll try to talk to her," Garner said. "I think I can convince her I was making up a story."

Chloe sniffed. "Oh, yeah, you're so persuasive."

"Well, she believed me before!"

"When you were telling her the truth."

"Stop it," Jude said again. "Just stop it. I'll

have to deal with this somehow, but I think a whole lot better when people aren't arguing."

The two of them fell silent at last. He gave an impatient huff of his own and started drumming his fingers again. "How long has she been in there?"

"Almost half an hour," Chloe said. "I tried to talk her out."

"Okay. Give her a little longer. At some point she's going to start wearing down and then I'll go in."

"Maybe I should go in with you," Chloe said.

"At this point I don't think she'll trust you too much, either. You're such an *inventive* liar, remember?"

Chloe scowled at him.

He sat motionless, waiting for time to pass, ignoring Chloe and Garner who were tossing glares at each other like ping-pong balls.

Finally, he stood. He had to go in there, and as near as he could determine, there was only one way to handle it.

After swiping his key card, he punched in

his code and listened to the dead bolts snap back. Then he walked into his office.

He faced a woman holding a sword in both hands. The hysteria had obviously passed to be replaced by determination and desperation. A lot easier to deal with.

She backed away from him until she could back up no farther. He left the door open, walked to the opposite side of the room and leaned back against the credenza, folding his arms.

"That's a good sword," he remarked. "I wore it on parade, even had to use it a few times at Waterloo."

"Stay away from me." Her voice trembled with intensity. And she still smelled so tempting.

"I have no intention of getting any closer. I just want to know one thing."

"What?"

"Why you ran in here instead of running out of the building."

She froze, biting her lip, then glared at him again. "I was frightened."

"Well, I can understand that. The door's

open. Run any time you want. No one will stop you. Just, please, leave my sword behind. It's one of my few keepsakes."

But she stood there, anyway, legs braced, still waving the sword although her arms must be getting weary. "Is it true?" she demanded.

"Is what true?"

"That you're a…a…" She apparently couldn't bring herself to say the word.

"I'm a vampire," he said, keeping his voice calm, even pleasant. "Yes, it's true."

"And you kill people?"

"I haven't killed anyone in a very long time who didn't deserve it. I don't kill just to feed."

A disbelieving sound escaped her.

He shrugged. "I don't need much, you know. A blood bank will take more from you than I will."

Something in her face was changing. Her mouth opened a little. Was he seeing the dawn of curiosity? He hoped so.

"Mostly," he said, "I buy blood. But I never dine without permission."

With that her jaw did drop open, and with it

the sword lowered. "You're lying," she whispered.

"Why would I lie? I just told you I'm a vampire. And you don't have anything to fear from me. If you did, I'd have fed on you last night. Because let me tell you, Terri, you smell that good to me."

The sword tip touched the floor, but she still looked ready to bolt. More important, he could see questions starting to swirl behind her eyes. Maybe they could get through this. If not, oh, well. No one would believe she'd met a real vampire, and if she grew too insistent, she might even get herself committed. He hoped she didn't go that route.

"Why…" Her whisper broke.

"Why what?"

She shook her head, still staring at him.

"You ought to sit," he suggested gently. "You've had a shock. I'll just stay over here and you can take that chair right by the door."

But she still didn't move. She just kept staring at him, and he could almost see mental furniture being rearranged behind her eyes.

"You're a ruthless killer," she finally said.

"Only when I have to be."

"What's that supposed to mean? What kind of excuse is that?"

"Would you kill to save your own life? Isn't that what you were thinking about doing with that sword? Isn't that what happened last night with Sam?"

She gasped, and a spark of something flared in her eyes. "Did you kill him?"

"Sam? No. I'll admit I would have liked to, but no. I warned him away. I threatened him. But I didn't even hit him."

A shudder passed through her. Dragging the sword, she eased her way to the chair and sat. He managed to suppress a wince at the way she treated that beautiful piece of steel.

"I can't believe this," she muttered.

"It would be nice if that were true," he agreed. "Unfortunately, you already believe it or you wouldn't have reacted the way you did. So here we are. You know my secret. You can leave. Or you can stay."

Her head shot up. "Why would I want to stay?"

"Apparently, you didn't want to leave. I

don't know why. Maybe you don't, either. And maybe you'd stay because you have more questions. It's entirely up to you."

Her eyes narrowed dubiously. "You're just saying that. You can't let me go now that I know."

He couldn't quite suppress a smile, recognizing that she was still having trouble coping with the fact that he was a vampire, and equally so with the notion that he intended her no harm. People often got repetitious as they struggled to accept a truth that violated their notions of reality. "Just who is going to believe you? A hundred years ago you might have been able to assemble a mob to come get me, but these days…" He shrugged.

"So nothing can hurt you?"

"Plenty can."

"Like what?"

He shook his head slowly and this time he did smile. "We're not intimate enough to share those secrets."

She leaned forward, putting weight on the sword point and finally he couldn't keep silent.

"Don't lean on it that way. Please. You'll damage it."

At once she straightened. "Why is it so important to you?"

"Because I carried it through an entire war. It saved me from serious trouble a time or two."

"How is that possible? You're immortal!"

"No one is immortal. I'll even die of old age. Eventually. If I survive long enough. Unlike you, I can die more than once."

"This is too much." She shook her head several times, as if she wanted to deny what she was thinking, or what he was saying.

He remained still and silent. His primary concern was to get her past this shock. Then she could leave, try to pick up her life, and one of these days she'd probably even convince herself she had imagined all of this because it simply wouldn't fit in her world.

Eventually, she spoke again. "If I struck you with this sword, what would happen?"

"You'd hurt me. You'd cut through flesh and maybe bone, depending on how hard you swing."

"And then?"

"And then I'd heal, the way I've been healing for nearly two hundred years, and by tomorrow night you wouldn't even be able to tell you'd done it."

She lowered the sword then, laying it on the rug. The eyes she raised to him looked pained. "I can't protect myself from you, can I?"

"Yes, you can. You can walk out. At any time."

"But why?" she asked plaintively. "Why would you let me go?"

Damn the movies, damn the myths and damn Bram Stoker. He invariably had an uphill battle against those deeply ingrained stories, on the rare occasions he acknowledged the truth of his mere existence.

"Because—" and this time his voice held a note of steel, mainly because her scent was getting to him again, and self-control, long nurtured, was fraying a bit "—I have absolutely no desire to harm you in any way."

"But that's what vampires do!"

"Not this one." He turned his head toward

the door and barked, "Chloe. Garner. Get in here."

The two appeared instantly as if they had been listening.

He glowered at them. "Are you undead?"

"Cripes," said Garner. "Do I look like it?"

Chloe loosed a huge sigh. "No."

"Not vampires?"

"Ugh," said Garner. "I practically faint at the sight of blood." He almost looked shame-faced.

"I'm certainly not," said Chloe.

"Have I ever harmed either of you? Stolen your blood?"

A chorus of nos.

"What would you say if I asked if I could feed?"

Garner paled. "Oh, jeez, Jude, you know I like you, man, but that? I don't think so."

"Chloe?"

"I'd say yes, but nobody's asking." She tossed her head.

Jude looked at Theresa. "There you go. And now I've got a job to do, one that's already been put on hold, so I'm leaving now."

Garner brightened. "Can I come, too?"

"After what you pulled tonight, I'm thinking about getting you a gag and a leash. Did you find out anything today?"

Garner shook his head. "Still only the two cases we know about. But I still have the other half of the city to do."

"Okay. Now, I'm going to give you some instructions and you're going to follow them to the letter."

Garner nodded eagerly.

"Stay here. Apologize to Terri for scaring her half to death. Apologize to Chloe for upsetting her. And then sit here and think about what possible earthly use you can be if all you do is give me headaches."

Jude crossed the room swiftly, not bothering to conceal his speed, picked up the sword and restored it to its place of honor on the wall.

"See you by dawn," he said, and was gone.

Theresa didn't move for a long time. She sat on the chair, staring blankly at the back of Jude's office. Chloe spoke to her a few times, even offered her a cup of tea, but she didn't answer.

A vampire.

Everything inside her rebelled at the thought now that the earlier terror had passed, now that she'd had that oddly calm conversation with Jude who had actually admitted, *admitted,* that he was a vampire.

But there weren't any vampires. Except... Except... He moved too fast. He had made those guys leave simply by telling them to go. His eyes changed color. And clearly both Garner and Chloe believed it was true.

She had either stumbled into a group of lunatics or... Her mind balked again. He moved too fast. She had seen it just a little while ago, when he had taken the sword and put it back on the wall. He had moved so fast that she hadn't seen him at all until he stopped to replace the sword. All she had felt was the breeze of his passage.

And no matter how she tried to reconstruct it, she couldn't see Jude where her mind had not seen him.

"Terri? Terri."

At long last she blinked and looked at Chloe.

"We need to get to the station and look at the mug shots. We promised Detective Matthews, remember?"

Feeling stiff, and not at all like herself, Terri followed Chloe to her car, a considerably nicer model than what Jude drove.

"You look like you're still in shock," Chloe remarked as they pulled away from the curb.

"Maybe I am."

"Believing in vampires is hard at first."

"That's just it. I don't."

Chloe's jaw dropped and she hit the brake, pulling over to the curb. Once she parked, she turned to face Terri. "Girl, you were threatening to kill the man. You were terrified. What do you mean, you don't believe it?"

"I don't know what came over me," Terri said, still feeling wooden and numb. "It was like I was possessed or something."

"Hey, we at Messenger Investigations don't joke about that." A pause, then "What do you mean? I don't get it."

Terri finally looked straight at her. "I don't get it, either. I can't believe I believed Garner.

I can't believe I was waving a sword at Jude. I can't believe my whole reaction. That wasn't like me. I'm a scientist. Give me physical evidence or I don't buy it. I must have had some kind of break."

Chloe opened her mouth then shut it, apparently reconsidering her words. "Okay."

"Okay?"

"Most people rationalize it away. Why should you be any different?"

"I'm not rationalizing. I wasn't myself and that scares me a bit."

"Whatever it takes to make you feel better. Even if that means you think we're all either crazy or lying."

Terri winced at Chloe's tone, and fell silent again as Chloe pulled them away from the curb and drove to the police station.

Did she think they were lying to her? No. But the only other explanations were equally unpalatable. They didn't seem like lunatics. Maybe it was some kind of reinforced delusion among the three of them?

But she kept coming back to the way Jude had moved too fast to see, the way his eyes changed. God, she needed an answer, a solid answer.

At the station they spent the next three hours going through an endless stream of mug shots. Terri felt wearier by the minute, until finally her eyes began to blur with fatigue. And she didn't recognize a single one of them.

Back in the car, Chloe steered them back to the office.

"Just take me home, Chloe," she asked quietly. "I've had enough. I'm exhausted."

"No."

"No? Why not? Do you want me to get a cab?"

"No. Dammit. You need to see Jude."

That woke Terri up. "What in the world for?"

"You'll see," Chloe said darkly.

"Just take me home!"

"I will after you see Jude. You want answers. Well, guess what. Now I want them, too."

"What kind of answers do *you* want?"

Chloe didn't answer, and short of diving out of a moving vehicle to land on empty streets in the wee hours, Terri had no choice. And after what had happened to her just last night on these streets, she wasn't inclined to be alone out here.

Jude emerged from his inner office only moments after she and Chloe stepped inside. The instant he saw Terri, he stiffened. "You?"

"Her," Chloe said. "We want some answers."

"Answers? To what?"

Chloe stepped forward, dragging an unhappy Terri with her. "This one," she said, indicating Terri with a jerk of her head, "doesn't believe you're a vampire."

"So?"

"So why did she get so scared and come after you like that?"

The question arrested Jude. He stood as still as a statue, staring at Terri.

"She says she felt possessed."

Jude drew a sharp breath. Before Terri could even register that he moved, he stood in front of her, inhaling deeply, studying her with intent, dark eyes. She wanted to pull back, but felt frozen.

"No," he said after a moment. "A hint of something…but no, she's not possessed."

"Okay then," Chloe continued doggedly. "You might not care what she thinks of you, but as it happens, I do. And I care what she thinks about me, too. We are not liars and we are not crazy."

Jude stepped back, giving Terri room to breathe. "What do you want?"

Terri shook her head. "Nothing. I'm sorry, this wasn't my idea. I didn't want to come here and accuse anyone of anything."

"Yes, you did," Chloe retorted. "Get some gumption." The she looked at Jude. "It's too much. You should have seen her sitting there after you left. I couldn't even get her to answer me for nearly an hour."

Terri was starting to feel awful. Regardless of what she felt, she hadn't meant to insult anyone, and now here she was indirectly insulting two people who had come to her rescue. "It's okay," she said desperately. "It doesn't matter what I believe."

"But it does," Chloe said. "If it gives you

mental peace, it matters. Even if you still want to think I'm a liar."

Terri's throat tightened at that generous statement.

"What am I missing here?" Jude asked. He looked at Terri. "What exactly is the problem?"

"It's my problem."

"Just tell me."

Terri drew a deep breath. She could hardly bear to look at either of them. "It's just that… I'm a forensic pathologist. By training and inclination, I never leap to conclusions. Everything must be based on evidence. *Everything*. People's lives depend on it. So I can't imagine why I believed Garner at all. I can't believe the way I reacted. And then I accepted it when you simply told me it was true."

"Identity crisis," Chloe said. "For the love of heaven, Jude, just make the woman whole."

"How the hell am I supposed to do that? I can certainly understand why she doesn't want to believe this."

Chloe spoke succinctly. "Prove it."

Chapter 4

Jude had been in better moods. The man he was after, the guy who was oppressed by demons, had moved on, and somehow he'd done it without leaving a trail. And now it was just before dawn, and Jude had returned as the vanquished rather than the victor.

And it galled him in part because except for intrusive events, such as rescuing a damsel in distress, he'd have already dealt with the problem. Now he was back at square one, and worse, it would require depending on Garner again.

After this night, he really didn't want to depend on Garner for anything.

And now this? "Proof?" he said incredulously.

Chloe nodded.

He turned to Terri. "Why the hell don't you just let this go? Just walk away and forget it all." *Walk away and save me from myself.* But he couldn't add that.

"I can't. I'm a scientist. A medical doctor. And if it's true…well, I need to know. I can't live with unanswered questions. I just can't."

"What do you want me to do? Feed on you?"

She blinked. "No."

"Oh, you want something more dramatic." He snarled, extending his fangs.

She shook her head. My God, he thought, she was crazy. Nuts. Something in her had snapped.

"Fangs," she said, "can be fake."

"Oh, for the love of…" He stopped. He was tired. The approaching dawn was prickling the back of his neck like mad. He was annoyed. He was irritated beyond belief that his mission had been stymied.

He was also failing to consider that this woman might need her proof simply for her own peace of mind. Yes, she was a scientist, and her damn science said he couldn't possibly be a vampire. He didn't exactly care for such ambiguities himself.

He muttered an oath. Okay then. He'd give her the proof, she could go home comfortable that she knew the truth, and probably by this time tomorrow night she'd have convinced herself it was all some kind of dream, anyway.

But whatever it took, because if he didn't get her out of here soon, he wasn't sure his self-control would survive. He wanted to have sex with her. He wanted to taste her. He wanted too damn much. So just do whatever it took to make her leave.

"Come into my office." He moved so swiftly he had to rely on the sound of her reluctant footsteps to be sure she followed him.

He went to the credenza and pulled out a dagger given to him long ago by a friend. It was an ornamental piece, but it was sharp. Too irritated to fuss with buttons, he ripped the front of his shirt open, baring his chest.

"Here's your proof," he said. With the dagger, he gashed his own chest.

She gasped and clapped a hand to her mouth. The blood hardly started to pour before the wound began to close up. She watched, her eyes growing even larger, until it closed completely, leaving only a faint scar that would be gone by nightfall.

"Now," he said, tossing the dagger on his desk, "I am going to bed, and you are going home."

Without another word, he turned, unlocked his bedroom, slipped inside and locked it behind him.

For a few moments he leaned against the door. Unbelievable, he thought. Unbelievable that she had wanted proof, and even more so that he had provided it.

He was losing it, he thought as he yanked his clothes off. Losing it. All because that woman's scent was headier than cocaine to an addict.

He wanted her gone. Now.

He grabbed some blood from his fridge,

downed it without tasting it, then crawled under the sheets as the prickling grew.

Every morning, he died again. And no one but he knew how much he hated it sometimes.

Theresa almost called in sick. Two nights without regular sleep had left her wasted. Her eyes felt grainy, her brain seemed to be bobbing on a sea of disconnected thoughts.

But she was still the newbie, and she didn't want to test Dr. Crepo's kindness. She took a quick shower and dressed in stylish casual clothes that would be replaced at work by scrubs. A glance in the mirror told her she looked as if her blood *had* been drained.

Oh, man, she was still having trouble with that. Jude Messenger was a vampire. An honest-to-God walking undead. What did that mean? Reality seemed to be lying in tatters around her feet, and she didn't know how to reassemble it. Worse, scientific curiosity seemed to be rearing up, demanding answers for how such a thing could be.

Answers she was certain she would never get, a true irony considering that she had wanted proof in order to answer questions. Why hadn't she realized that if he actually proved to her that he was a vampire that she'd only have more maddening questions? Maybe because somewhere inside she'd been sure he wouldn't be able to prove it, leaving her with no questions at all.

Ghosts she could deal with. She had lived in a haunted house through much of her childhood, and experience had knitted that possibility into her reality. But a *vampire?*

And certainly not what she would have expected of one. A *vampire* had saved her from rape. Possibly from death. He'd extended her every courtesy. He'd even given her the proof she needed, and now when she thought about that, she almost squirmed.

She wasn't in the habit of making people do extraordinary things to prove they were who they said they were.

Lord, did he even rate as *people?* As human?

There were no boxes for this one, and for the first time in her life she faced her need for pigeonholes. A way to classify everything. Boxes, labels, stereotypes.

He broke all of them wide open.

Even at work, trying to focus on a prelim, all she had to do was summon an image of Jude to feel again that pull, that attraction. As if he were a magnet and she a pile of iron filings. Her mind kept wandering down sexually imaginative corridors, wondering what it would be like to kiss him, to feel those steely arms wrapped around her. Did he even make love the way humans did? Could he?

What was *that?* How could she feel so drawn to something that was inhuman? Dead? Whatever.

He sure didn't seem dead. She knew death intimately in its many forms, in fact was even now examining a body for every mark, cut, scratch or puncture, even though it was obvious this man had died by gunshot, or in the overworn joke: he'd died from lead poisoning.

Jude might be *un*dead, but he was certainly not dead-dead. He had bled. She had seen it with her own two eyes. Not nearly what she would have expected from a human with a gashed chest, but he had bled.

So what did that mean? His heart pumped. He talked, he walked, he smiled, even laughed, and he could certainly get grumpy.

And he had saved her life, not taken it.

As she made notes on the clipboard on a steel table not far from Case Number HD-451036, aka Daniel Subo, she put her forehead in her hand, feeling as if the ground reeled beneath her feet.

"You don't look good."

She lifted her head and stared blankly at her boss, Dr. Crepo. "Sorry, I had trouble sleeping last night."

He shook his head sympathetically. "It hasn't been that long since you were attacked. Take some time, Terri."

"I... Well, I guess I don't want to give in."

He sighed. "Sometimes you have to. The mind needs healing as much as the body. Time to deal with things. And I don't want you messing something up."

If she went home she'd just have that much more time to think. To beat her head against an impossibility that had become all too real. The thought filled her with dread. "You're right, but…"

"You don't want to be alone, do you?"

"Not really."

"Can't risk the mistakes," he said firmly. "Finish those notes, then go out for dinner with a friend or something. Right now you look a hundred years old."

That mention carried her directly back to Jude. *Nearly two hundred years?* He'd said that, hadn't he? And stuff about fighting at Waterloo?

Another shudder ripped through her, and she tried to focus all of her attention on the document on the clipboard. Post mortems were so orderly in so many ways. And when a puzzle turned up, it was fascinating, not frightening.

Too bad life couldn't be tied up so neatly.

She managed to get the priority stuff finished by four. Then she went home and collapsed in her bed, telling herself she would sleep through the entire night, wake up in the morning and find that everything had returned to normal.

Yeah, sure.

Instead she had crazy dreams, dreams of the ghost from her childhood, dreams of Jude leaning close and murmuring, "I want to taste you." And when she dreamed that last one she jerked awake in a state of full arousal and sexual hunger.

That made her so mad she beat her fist on her pillow a couple of times before trying to settle down again.

She couldn't possibly really want that…that *vampire*. There was something totally wrong about that. It had to be wrong.

Didn't it?

Of course it was wrong, which explained why she climbed into a cab at two in the morning and headed for Jude's office.

Something still needed settling so that she could get back into her life. Something. If only she knew exactly what. Compulsion seemed to be goading her, and in some corner of her mind she knew that wasn't normal. Her only compulsion extended to accuracy in her work.

This was weird, but she could no longer fight it off.

She had to ring the bell at Jude's front door. Chloe's voice answered promptly. "Messenger Investigations. Can I help you?"

"It's me, Chloe."

Silence. "I was hoping that wasn't you I was looking at on the CCTV."

Before Terri could answer, she heard a buzz and the door unlocked. She walked into the dark hallway and closed the door behind her. Then down the hall a door opened and Chloe peered out.

"What is it with you, Terri? Do you want to drive the guy nuts?"

"I'm the one who is going nuts." Terri walked down the hall and entered Chloe's office. Garner wasn't there, and that relieved her somehow. "How could I possibly drive *him* nuts?"

"Did you hear what he said last night?"

"He said a lot."

Chloe frowned and returned to her desk. She didn't say anything for a moment, then picked up a pencil and began rapping it on the desk. "You really don't get it."

"Get what?"

"He said you smell that good to him."

"So?"

Chloe dropped the pencil and leaned forward. "Imagine a starving man faced with a banquet table. Jude limits himself almost entirely to canned blood. He's the starving man. And you're the banquet."

Shock shook Terri, but the feeling that accompanied it wasn't entirely unpleasant. That should scare her, but it didn't.

"You're fascinated," Chloe said.

"I guess so. Did he do that to me?"

"He can't help it. Some people feel it more than others. I felt it." She shrugged. "Thank God it wears off. But he never told me I smelled good to him. So maybe you ought to be smart and walk out of here. Because even Jude must have limits to his self-control. I haven't found them yet, but they must be there."

"Why does he limit himself?"

Chloe sighed and sagged back into her chair.

"You know, I never ask him questions like that."

"Why not?"

"Because it occurs to me that a guy who's been a vampire for nearly two hundred years, and who put in a good thirty before that as a mortal, must have had plenty of time to figure things out, and reasons for them, and it's none of my business. He shares what he chooses and I leave it at that."

"But don't you ever wonder?"

Chloe shook her head. "His business. I watch him fight every single day for good things. What more do I need to know?"

But something in Terri wouldn't leave it at that. "Is he out?"

"Yes."

"Doing what?"

"He has a case."

"What kind of case?"

Chloe scrunched up her face. "You don't take a brush-off very well. I can't discuss case details with you. You don't work here. Can't you just go home, be grateful and leave it at that? Because believe me, you don't want to get any deeper into this."

"Into what?"

Chloe hesitated, obviously thinking. Choosing words. Terri wondered if she would hear another lie. But then Chloe sighed, and there was something so open in her face, that Terri knew she was about to hear the truth.

"Remember your reaction to finding out Jude is a vampire?"

"How could I forget?"

"Then multiply it. Because there are far worse things out there than even a vampire running amok."

A chill touched Terri's neck. "Like what?"

Chloe hesitated again then said, "Let me give you the short version. Then maybe you'll have the good sense to go home."

"Maybe." Terri wasn't making any promises.

"Demons," Chloe said flatly. "Evil. Real, true evil. You don't have to believe me. I don't care if you do. But Jude hunts them and gets rid of them. Garner helps, insofar as Garner is ever capable of helping with anything, because he has a gift for sensing them. So Jude is a demon slayer, Garner is a demon hunter, and me…I'm just the jack-of-all-trades and defender of the office gate. Oh, and researcher when necessary."

"Oh." Terri's mind balked again, but not as long this time. A picture was emerging in her mind and amazingly enough, she believed it. "I lived in a haunted house."

"Meaning?" Chloe looked curious.

"I know there's supernatural stuff. And not all of it is good."

"Trust me, Terri, no ghost could prepare you for what Jude fights."

"Maybe not. But I'm not going to sit here and dismiss what you're saying."

Chloe raised a brow. "I guess that means you're not leaving?"

"No."

"Well, don't be surprised if Jude blows right by you into his bedroom. He never comes home from one of these things in a good mood."

"I don't care."

"And I can't figure you out."

"I can't, either," Terri admitted.

Chloe expelled a noisy sigh. "It's your head. Or whatever. Well, if you're going to be sitting here for hours, you can help me."

"Doing what?"

"Some research."

Which was how Terri came to be reading M.E.'s reports, and since the cases apparently weren't closed, she was quite certain she was doing something illegal, even if she herself had legal access. Her access came by virtue of her job, but Jude shouldn't have access at all.

But Jude apparently could access quite a database of them online. Maybe he had special permission.

She didn't want to know how he got it, or whether he really had it.

She just kept reading, growing increasingly fascinated herself. She never would have guessed how many murders there had been in this city of several million over the last year, or how many of them had oddities. Teeth marks, claw marks, ritual markings.

Of course, most of the deaths were from natural causes, but eventually she had printed out eight of them as being the unusual kind of thing Chloe said she was looking for.

And just as she was handing them over to Chloe, Jude walked in.

"You?" he said, sounding astonished.

"Her," Chloe said. "Where's Garner?"

"I sent him home for some sleep."

"No luck?"

"No. It's like word went out on a grapevine or something." He was talking to Chloe, but he was looking at Terri. She felt herself flush faintly.

Chloe took the papers from her. "She's been helping with research."

Jude was still staring at her from those dark eyes. "Why?"

Terri shrugged.

Something in his dark eyes hardened. Then he snatched the papers from Chloe's hand and vanished into his office so quickly Terri never saw him move. She knew only where he had gone because she heard the dead bolts snap into place.

Chloe shrugged at her. "What did I tell

you? He won't be back out until sunset, so you might as well go home."

But before the words were barely out of her mouth, the *thunk* of dead bolts alerted them, and suddenly Jude was standing there in the doorway. And he was looking at Terri.

"Come in here," he said.

Every instinct warned her not to. But something deeper called her. Slowly she walked toward him and entered his office. Her neck prickled when she heard him close the door behind her. No bolts. He just closed it.

The next thing she knew, he was standing behind her and she could feel the whisper of his breath on her neck. Not warm breath, like a human's, but cool. A shiver ran through her, a surprisingly pleasant one. Arousal gripped her instantly, a sweet clenching that caused her to feel breathless.

"Don't you get it?" he whispered, and then inhaled so deeply she felt he was drawing her into his lungs.

"Get what?" she whispered back.

"I'm a vampire. I want you like hell on fire. And you're on thinner ice than you can possibly know." He breathed deeply again, then almost instantaneously reappeared in the chair behind his desk, leaving space between them.

"Sit," he said, pointing to one of the armchairs that faced his desk.

She obeyed, slowly, never taking her eyes from him.

"Why?" he asked.

"I don't know."

He studied her, frowning. "Maybe you better figure it out before you come back here again. You want me to feed on you? I can do that. I'll also give you a sexual rush you'll never forget. But the danger is…" He paused.

"You might not be able to stop?"

"No. I can stop. I never let myself get so hungry I can't stop. The danger is, you might want more of it. You might never be able to forget it, and nothing will ever be quite as good."

"Seriously?" Astonishment caused her heart to trip.

"Seriously." His smile was grim. "How do you think we survive? Not by causing pain and horror, at least not usually."

"Oh." She hadn't thought of that.

"Which is not to say I couldn't. I could scare you out of here in the next ten seconds in a way that would ensure you never set foot here again."

"Then why don't you?"

"Damned if I know." He continued to study her, frowning. Her heart pounded heavily, but only slightly faster than normal. She felt as if she stood on the lip of a precipice of some kind but couldn't back away.

Finally, he rose and went into the room beyond. She caught a glimpse of his bedroom, just a glimpse before he returned carrying a bag she recognized instantly as blood.

"I buy this from a blood bank," he said, holding up the bag. "A fresh delivery every three days. It's awful."

"Why?"

"Because it's full of anticoagulants. It's like drinking rotgut wine when you know a bottle of the really fine stuff is within reach."

That actually struck her as sad. The reaction shocked her, and made her wonder yet again about her own state of mind. Sympathizing with a vampire? But she did. "That's awful."

He shrugged. "You deal with what is."

Then, astonishing her with the bluntness of his act, he bared his fangs, plunged them into the bag, and began to drink. After a few gulps he looked at her with red-rimmed lips. "*This* is reality."

She swallowed hard, but refused to stop watching as he drained the bag. When he was done, he tossed it aside and pulled a tissue from the box on his desk and wiped his mouth.

"Feeling sick yet?" he asked.

"No." And she wasn't. She'd dealt with enough blood and gore that the only thing that could surprise her was that someone could drink that much blood without getting ill. She couldn't even feel shock.

"Reality is that I die every morning. I can fight the sun for a little while in here, where it can't reach me, but not for too long. So I die every morning. And when darkness returns, I resurrect. I have only half a life, sometimes even less than that. There was a time I was an indiscriminate killer because I had to feed, and I couldn't leave anyone behind to tell what had happened. Then I learned. I learned self-control. I mastered my compulsion. I found ways to handle it."

"Why?"

"Because I loathed myself. Do you think I wanted to become *this?*"

Surprisingly, she ached for him. She couldn't imagine living with so much self-hatred. "I'm sorry. How did it happen?"

He hesitated, his eyes darker than ever. The light in here was dim. Just enough for her to see by.

"Because of an act of kindness."

"What?" It didn't seem to connect.

"Before the battle at Waterloo. I saw a woman being harassed one night by some drunken soldiers. I intervened. I thought I was saving her from them."

"No?"

He shook his head. "I had no way to guess that the only thing I saved her from was having to reveal what she really was. She wouldn't have let them hurt her. In the end, they would probably all have been dead, but I didn't know that. I guess I really saved *them,* even though I had the provosts arrest them. But I didn't know."

"How could you?"

"It doesn't matter. After the battle…" He closed his eyes. "The dead. There were so many. Thousands upon thousands. And the survivors lay among them, hard to find in the carnage. I was badly wounded. Dying. I vaguely remember lying there all night and through the next day, listening to moans, drifting in and out of consciousness. I didn't care. I just wanted death to end it all. I could feel the gangrene beginning. It was worse than the pain from the musket ball."

Terri had enough medical experience to imagine what it had been like, and the image was still terrible enough to make her hurt with horror for him. Never in her life had she considered what it must be like to be wounded, and lying hopelessly among the dead and screaming. Her experience had taken her to some pretty awful places, but none on that scale.

"Anyway," he continued, "she found me.

That woman I thought I had saved. And she saved *me*. She dragged me out of that stinking heap of carnage to her little house, and she turned me." His gaze grew distant, as he lost himself in memory.

Terri remained quiet, absorbing the things he was telling her, accepting the truth of them at last. At least she accepted the emotional truth. The scientist in her was far from happy. Finally, she asked, "Are you grateful to her?"

His dark eyes snapped back to her. "Once in a while. It was a difficult transition. I couldn't go back to my family and friends. I had to learn a whole new way of life, one that repelled me even as all my newborn instincts demanded I do those things. All in all, it was an ugly time. I was filled with rage beyond description. I should have just died, but when I demanded to know how I could end it all, she just laughed at me and told me I'd get used to it."

The impulse to comfort him nearly overwhelmed her, but there didn't seem to be anything she could say or do. Not one darn thing.

"Enough of that," he said abruptly. "I'm

here. Still. Sometimes I even revel in the night. Nothing is all bad, not even being a vampire. But it does make me dangerous, Terri. Especially to someone like you. I'm a predator. I'll always be a predator. I can control it, but I can't change it. You need to understand that. Believe it. And get the hell out."

It was then that Terri understood at last at least part of what was driving her. She bit her lip, then decided to just say it out loud. "You may be a predator, but you saved my life."

"Maybe. Or maybe I saved your virtue. They might not have killed you."

"You saved me from more than that. You saved me from a gang rape, from a beating. I could be in the hospital or the morgue right this instant."

He waved his hand as if it was meaningless now.

"You saved me," she said again. "Then you took care of Sam so I don't have to be afraid of him anymore. I owe you."

"You don't owe me a thing."

"Yes. I do." And that was why she kept coming back, at least part of what she was struggling with. "Unfinished business," she said.

"No, it's finished."

"It's not. I owe you. I want to repay you. I always pay my debts."

"Don't be ridiculous!"

"I always pay my debts. It's how I was raised. I'll pay your fee gladly."

"I don't want your money."

She closed her eyes and drew a long, shaky breath, terrified of the impulse that was growing in her, but unable to squash it. "You want my blood."

"I'm not hungry." He sounded angry.

"You want my blood, anyway. So just take it. I owe you."

"Not that." His voice was as hard and sharp as the edge of a blade.

"Yes. If not tonight…" She opened her eyes. "Then another time. It's the least I can do to thank you."

His glare was truly frightening, almost wild with anger. "The last woman who thought she needed to repay me turned me into a monster."

He was gone before she could blink, his

destination revealed only by the closing of his bedroom door.

She sat there, shaking, feeling weak, scarcely believing what she had just offered. Yet, was it so different from a blood donation? And if that was the only way she could repay him…

A long time later, on rubbery knees, she managed to stand and walk out. She barely murmured good-night to a puzzled Chloe.

Out on the street, she found sunlight painting the world golden. She hailed a cab and headed home to get ready for yet another day at work.

Okay, she told herself. She had offered to pay her debt in the coin he would most value. He hadn't accepted it. But at least she had offered. Maybe that sense of debt unpaid had been what had been making her feel so uneasy, like something was hanging over her head. Like something was tagging along with her. It certainly seemed to be gone now.

Now, perhaps, she could forget the whole thing. Perhaps now she could go back to her world of science, and solve problems that could be solved, and pigeonhole things that could be pigeonholed.

Because she desperately needed to do exactly that.

Chapter 5

Something was watching her, following her. The awareness rode Terri constantly again, reminding her awfully of her childhood. Scaring her. Plaguing her. As much as she tried to ignore the feeling, she couldn't quite banish it. Apparently, she'd been mistaken that it had arisen from her sense of unfinished business with Jude.

Yes, it seemed to have begun right around the time Jude had saved her. Or just after. After she left his office for the last time. But evidently she'd mistaken its cause, because even though she had offered to repay him somehow, the feeling had returned. Stronger now.

God, she thought she'd left that sensation behind years ago, the night she stopped panicking and got mad, and hunted up the family Bible that nobody in her house ever looked at, and added the St. Michael prayer from the back of a holy card a friend had given her.

Her religious training had been minimal, something her family had treated as an identifier, not a practice. But her girlfriend, Tina, had come to her rescue with advice and the holy card.

And one night she had gotten fed up with the voice, with the watcher, with the whole damn thing. Anger had triumphed over terror, and she'd stood in her bedroom all alone with just a penlight, and she had read the Psalm, then chanted the St. Michael prayer repeatedly, and demanded that ghost get out of her house, out of her life.

To this day she remembered the shadow that had seemed to rise from one corner of her room, darker than the darkness of the unlighted room, as if in defiance. How her heart had tripped at the sight. How her anger had risen to her support, making her pray even more loudly.

The thing had vanished and never returned.

But now here she was again, sixteen years later, with that same creepy, awful feeling of being watched.

And now she had come to hate the way her shift often made her go home after dark, because she often stayed late to finish important details while they were fresh in her mind.

It was an odd schedule, designed to introduce her to everyone on the M.E.'s team regardless of their shifts, an opportunity for her to learn from everyone. But because it was a shift designed just for her, she was seriously beginning to think of asking Dr. Crepo to change it. Except how could she explain her request? She certainly couldn't say she felt as if some *thing* was following her, watching her.

She rode the bus home with a headache. Sometimes she wondered if she had made a bad career choice, choosing to work with the dead, rather than the living. With the living she might have saved lives. With the dead she could do nothing but bear witness to what had happened to them. Yes, she knew she was giving voice to those whom death had left voiceless. But sometimes she found it a grim way to live. Maybe it was getting to her.

Leaning her head against the window, she waited for the blocks to pass, grateful for the coolness of the glass. Hoping that she'd make it into the safety of her apartment before something caught her, much as she had felt as a child. Again and again she told herself that was ridiculous, and tried to focus on reality. The real moments and events in her life.

As the bus started and stopped, she watched happier faces pass by, or even climb aboard, like the smiling mother with two excited children, both of whom seemed to be eagerly anticipating getting home to play with new toys. Had her life ever been that simple?

Not since she was five and had first experienced the prickling feeling that something was watching her. The feeling over the past week had grown so strong that now, when she got home in the evening, she stayed home, refusing to follow even her usual pursuits, like going to the gym.

Like back when she'd lived in the haunted house. Only different somehow. Inside her locked apartment, the feeling went away. It was only when she was out and about that she felt observed. She was growing increasingly unnerved, but without a thing to point to, what could she do?

Some little voice kept telling her to go to Jude with her concern. That he wouldn't dismiss her. But how could she know that when she hardly knew him at all?

A part of her felt sorry for him, because the more she thought about it, the more she realized that his life must be full of loss. If he made any friends, he outlived them. Everyone he cared about would slip away sooner or later.

Yet he still seemed to care. She could tell he cared about both Chloe and Garner, even though he could be tough on Garner. How could he keep opening himself to that loss over and over again?

It seemed he was courageous in more ways than one.

She sighed and closed her eyes for a minute, hoping the pounding in her head would ease, that her neck would stop prickling. She thought again of going to Jude.

Although he'd made it pretty clear he'd be happy if he never saw her again. Nor could she blame him. She'd been pretty selfish by persisting when he kept telling her to get lost, even when he warned her how much he wanted her and told her flat out he wouldn't cross that line with her.

She'd actually tormented him by offering her blood.

She was an idiot.

Sighing, she opened her eyes again and then stiffened.

There was Jude, standing on the sidewalk, ignoring the few people who hurried around him, looking up at a very low-rent apartment building. This could be a bad part of town, one she wouldn't have come through at all except for the bus.

At once she grabbed the cord to stop the bus. The driver obliged her half a block later. Almost frantically she hurried down the aisle, practically stumbling in her eagerness to get down the steps.

What was she doing? Even as she ran toward where she'd seen him, she scolded herself. He'd told her to get lost more than once. She must be nuts.

But as if something stronger than sense tugged at her, she kept going. And saw him enter the apartment building almost casually.

She burst into the small lobby in time to see the elevator doors close behind him. Impatiently she watched the display until she saw it stop on the seventh floor. Then she punched the button desperately, calling the cars back.

What was she doing? The question shrieked at the back of her brain but she ignored it. She didn't even answer the equally noisy question of what she was going to do if she found him. She knew, just *knew* that she had to follow him.

He'd probably be so mad at her...

The next car over arrived just a few seconds later. She stepped in alone and hit the button for the seventh floor. It seemed to take forever.

Then, finally, she arrived and stepped into a deserted hallway.

Brilliant, she thought. Absolutely brilliant. Had she really thought she'd find him dallying up here?

Just as she was about to summon the elevator again, to go home and take care of her pounding head, she heard his voice around a corner in the hallway. She couldn't make out the words, but there was no mistaking that it was him.

She hurried around the corner just in time to see the door close behind him as he stepped inside.

Now what? She could hear nothing, see nothing. She was being nosy, she had no business here, she must be out of her mind...

She pressed her ear to the door and heard something that made the hair on the back of her neck stand on end. Was that a growl?

Then Jude's voice. Chanting. Chanting in a cadence she remembered from childhood and movies. Latin?

A guttural scream, not even human she was sure. Heart pounding, she pulled back from the door and leaned against the wall. What was going on in there? That demon-fighting that Chloe had talked about?

Leave now.

That's what she should do. This could go on for hours, she didn't have any part in it. Yet she remained rooted as the minutes turned into nearly an hour, for some reason unable to run. Something compelled her to stay, much as she wanted to flee. Something seemed to have called her here, and she couldn't fight it.

Her heart wouldn't slow down, her breath kept coming rapidly, almost in pants, and she hardly noticed the one or two people who passed by and looked at her oddly. All she knew was that a force inside her refused to let her leave.

Then someone stuck his nose out of a nearby apartment and looked at her. "What's going on in there? Jeez, it sounds like a dog with rabies."

Terri stared at him, seeking words, any kind of explanation. Finally a lie sprang to her lips. "My friend's a dog trainer. He's trying to help with a troublesome dog."

The guy shook his head. "Dogs like that shouldn't be allowed. I'm going to complain to management."

"Just give my friend a chance first. He's really good with this stuff."

The guy hesitated, and the way his gaze swept over Terri told her he was responding more to the fact that she was an attractive young woman than anything she said.

"Okay," he finally grumped. "But another hour and I need to go to bed, and I *will* complain."

"Thanks. I'll tell my friend."

"Be sure you do."

When he closed his door, Terri once again closed her eyes, though not for long. Instead, fear began to creep slowly along her spine, then spread out to her very nerve endings. It had grown quieter in the apartment. Too quiet? How would she know?

But she felt something else. That feeling of being watched by some unseen presence returned suddenly. Only it was worse now, far worse. Her mouth turned dry as dust, and her palms grew damp. This presence held her rooted, forbidding her to run.

God, she hated this feeling.

Not knowing what else to do, she began to whisper the prayer she had memorized as a child to drive away whatever was inhabiting the house with her family. She prayed with every ounce of her being, pushing back at that sense of lurking evil. She must have said the prayer a hundred times as she stood there, her lips barely moving, her voice seemingly lost to her.

Suddenly, the door beside her opened. Before she knew what was happening, a hand grabbed her arm and she was dragged inside the apartment. The door slammed behind her and she felt herself in the unbreakable grip of a vampire.

Jude was glaring at her, but he was also weaving a bit. That's when she saw that his black shirt was ripped, and huge, blackened wounds crisscrossed his chest.

"My God," she whispered. "What happened?"

"I heard you out there. I could hear your

heartbeat, smell you. Damn it, Terri, do you have any idea of the risk? Of how much you could have distracted me?"

He sagged a little, releasing her, then took two steps toward an empty chair. He nearly fell into it.

Nearby, she saw another man, middle-aged, balding. He looked so pale and his eyes were closed.

"Is he…is he…?" The thought alone nearly made her heart stop.

"Dead? No. But the demon is gone. For now, anyway."

Her eyes snapped back to Jude. God, he looked awful. "Is it okay to tell a vampire he looks deader than usual?"

"Bloody hell," he muttered. "Humor at a time like this."

"What can I do? Will you heal? And oh, by the way, the guy next door says you have to be done here by eleven o'clock or he's calling management."

Jude rolled his eyes, then closed them for a second. When they snapped open, they were blacker than night. "See that plastic bottle over there?"

She looked where he pointed. It was a full liter bottle, but there was a cross on it. "Holy water?"

"Yeah. Pour a little of it on my chest, then pour some over him. Then shake what's left around all the doors and windows."

She did as told, as quickly as she could. Already Jude was healing, she saw, and the holy water seemed to speed the process. So he could tolerate holy water? Another myth bit the dust.

She came back to him with the empty bottle. "I've got to do something about those wounds." The doctor in her battled with another part that reminded her this guy wasn't human, and her arts and training probably wouldn't help him a bit. But she needed to do *something*.

He shook his head. "There's not a damn thing you can do. Now, help me button my coat. Then we're getting out of here."

She did as he asked, concealing the bloody, blackened wounds on his chest. He managed to get to his feet, but after only two steps, he stopped and put his arm around her shoulders, leaning heavily.

"Sorry," he said. "I need to feed. Soon."

"You can feed right now." The words came out of her on impulse. As soon as they escaped she felt a strange mix of shock and eagerness to give him what he needed. No different, she rationalized, than giving a patient a needed transfusion. Or maybe not. God, she hated this confusion. There was so much she desperately needed to understand.

"Damn it, no! Just help me get back to the office."

She got him downstairs in the elevator. When a man in the lobby started to look at them oddly, she even managed a little giggle and stood on tiptoe to kiss Jude on the cheek. To her surprise, while his skin was cooler than a human's, it wasn't the ice she expected. The man politely looked away and they escaped outside.

"My car's around the corner," Jude said.

Of course she recognized it. "Keys?"

"Top left pocket."

She felt around until she found them, by which time they reached the car. She unlocked the door and held it open for him. He slid in without argument, just put his head back against the headrest and let her drive.

He didn't even try to lecture her anymore. But if he had, she'd have given him a mouthful. What would he have done if she hadn't come along? Stayed there until he couldn't stay any longer, hoping to heal enough to get home on his own? Maybe.

"Do you need blood to heal?" she asked him.

"Sometimes."

"Tonight?"

"It'll help."

Not much of an answer.

Traffic steadily lightened, and they reached the office only a half hour later. Jude managed to get out of the car under his own steam. Terri trotted after him, determined not to let him out of her sight until she was sure he'd be okay.

He didn't argue with her. He used his key card to open the front door, and together they stepped into the darkened hallway. Terri couldn't see a thing, but Jude clapped a hand to her shoulder. Guiding her and leaning a little at the same time.

Then they reached the door of his office suite. It was she who reached out and turned the handle, throwing it open. Yellow light, welcome to her, filled the office. Garner was absent. Chloe was lying on the couch. Did she ever go home? Did she have a home?

Chloe sat up as soon as she heard them. Her sleepy eyes grew huge. "Oh, Jude," she said, somewhere between horror and annoyance.

"I just need to feed. Get me inside."

Chloe seemed to know exactly where to look for the key card for his office, and apparently she also knew the code to punch in.

Once in his office, Jude sagged into his chair. "Get me a bag," he said to Chloe.

A small refrigerator that Terri hadn't seen before now occupied a place near his desk. Chloe went to it immediately and pulled out a bag of blood.

Jude took it and ripped into it without even the little bit of finesse he'd shown just last week when he'd tried to make Terri feel revolted. He tipped back his head and poured the blood in as fast as he could swallow.

"Another?" Chloe asked.

"Not yet."

He started to unbutton his coat, but Terri could see that he was still weak and his hands shook. Impatiently, she brushed his hands aside and undid the buttons herself, revealing the wounds.

"They look better than they did when I first saw them," she remarked.

"Damn," Chloe said, seeing them for the first time. "What did he do to you?"

"A little of this and a little of that," Jude answered. Again, no answer at all.

Chloe put her hands on her hips. "You've got to stop doing this all alone."

"Apparently, I wasn't alone tonight," he answered. His eyes, not quite so dark now, trailed to Terri. "Don't do that again."

"I didn't do anything except help you get out of there," she argued hotly. "And a darn good thing I was there!"

"Amen to that," Chloe said with equal heat.

"You nearly distracted me. I can't be distracted when I'm dealing with a demon. I heard your heart. I smelled you. If I'd lost my concentration for even one second..."

He let the implied threat hang there. Then he sighed and let his head fall back, closing his eyes.

"Those wounds are healing awfully slowly," Chloe said.

"Damned canned blood," he remarked, as if that explained it all.

Terri looked at Chloe. "What's he mean?"

"The anticoagulants. And of course, the blood isn't fully alive anymore. So it's not quite the same."

"Oh. Well, he won't take *mine*." That kind of annoyed her actually, given his present state. "What, it's not good enough?"

"I think," said Chloe, "the problem is that it might be too good. Now stop harassing the man. He's got enough to deal with right now."

Terri fell silent, still annoyed, and inexplicably hurt, but realizing that she was probably being selfish again. Jude Messenger gave her a whole new definition to being selfish. But she'd sort that out later.

"Get me another one, Chloe. God, this hurts!"

"Like what?" Chloe asked as she brought him another bag.

"Fire. It's burning like fire."

"Demons," Chloe snapped. "What do you expect?"

"I don't need a mother."

"Yes, boss, actually you do."

Jude tore into the second bag, draining it. He didn't even wipe his mouth, so Terri dared to grab a tissue and dab away the drips herself.

"Stop hovering," he growled.

"Not until you start healing faster," Chloe argued.

"I probably won't heal completely before tomorrow night." He grimaced. "Demon wounds take longer. A lot longer."

"And you're planning to face two more of these by yourself?"

"Two more?" Terri was horrified.

"Two more," Chloe said grimly. "If we're lucky. I'm going to call Father Dan. You can't keep doing this alone."

"Let the man have his vacation! Damn it, Chloe, I can run my own life."

This time it was Terri who sniffed. "Oh, yeah, I can see that." She ignored his glare, and noted now that he'd had two full containers of blood, his eyes had turned almost golden. Like a wolf's or a tiger's.

"You're going to be the death of me," he said to her.

"I think it's too late for that."

He scowled but gave up the argument. "I can smell demon all over me. And my own rotting blood." He swore. "I gotta change."

"I'll get you a shirt," Chloe said. "The cleaners delivered this morning, so I don't need to invade your inner sanctum."

"Like I have one anymore."

Chloe rolled her eyes and looked at Terri. "I *told* you he always comes back from these things crabby." Then she flounced out to get the shirt.

Jude sat up and started peeling away his coat. Terri immediately leaned in to help, tugging it from his arms. For once he didn't give her a hard time. Then his shirt, pulling open the buttons down the front, the ones that still remained, undoing the cuffs. She helped him shrug it off, trying to ignore the occasional groan that escaped him.

She held up the tattered shirt. "Garbage?"

He waved to the red container by the fridge. "Biohazard container. I won't be able to stand the smell."

She flipped the latch and dropped the shirt in with the emptied blood bags.

When she turned around, he was standing, letting his leather coat fall to the floor.

"That, too?" she asked. Even wounded as he was, it was hard not to notice his perfect musculature. Did immortality confer that, too?

"No. Give it to Chloe. She'll bag it and send it to a cleaner. Ask her to empty the pockets."

She went to the outer office, where Chloe was looking through a stack of boxes with the name of a local dry cleaner stamped on them. "I don't even know if he should try to wear a shirt," she muttered. "He's a mess!"

"He wants this coat cleaned, too."

Chloe nodded. "I'll get a bag for it. Just empty his pockets."

So Terri did, feeling a little like she was prying, and winding up totally astonished by what she found in there. Not only things like keys, and key cards, and credit cards, but a rosary, a large crucifix, more holy water and a small red-covered copy of the *Roman Ritual for Exorcism*.

There went another myth, she thought, as she laid these things on Chloe's desk.

Chloe returned with a large garbage bag and together they stuffed the leather coat into it. "I'll take it to the cleaner's first thing in the morning."

Carrying a silk shirt, Chloe started back into Jude's office. Terri trotted after her.

Jude, however, was no longer there. Through the open door of the bedroom, they could see him lying on his bed, one arm thrown over his eyes.

"Just lock me in" was all he said when he heard them.

The two women exchanged glances. "Later," Chloe said. "You might need something."

"I need to teach you to follow orders."

"Someday. Good luck. I'll close this door at dawn, and not one second before."

He muttered something, and Terri suspected she should be glad she couldn't understand.

They walked out then, but left both doors open a crack. "In case he needs something," Chloe said.

Out in the front office, Chloe looking tired beyond words, and Terri feeling like it, they sat and simply looked at one another.

"Do you have a home to go to?" Terri asked finally.

"Yeah. Sometimes I even get there. But when we're on a case like this, I kind of camp out here."

"You look exhausted."

"I am." Chloe yawned. "But somebody needs to be here. It's not every day a demon messes him up like this. What if he needs something? What if he doesn't heal as fast as he expects?"

Terri hesitated. "I can stay. In fact, if you want, I can stay all day tomorrow."

"But what about your job?"

"I have tomorrow off."

Chloe cocked a brow at Terri. "How did you happen to be there?"

"I saw him on the street and followed. Don't even ask me why. It was just this feeling, that I had to."

Chloe yawned. "Well, I'm glad you were there, even if he wasn't. I keep telling him not to do this solo. He listens so well."

"So I gather."

All of a sudden, Chloe stood. "I'm going to trust you."

Terri felt her heart jump. "How so?"

"I'm going to go home. I need a shower. I need a bed. I need a decent night's sleep before I become the Wicked Witch of the East. Or was it the West? I'm too tired to remember." She shrugged.

"You can trust me."

Chloe smiled wearily. "I honestly think I can. So here's the deal. You wait until dawn. Make sure he doesn't need anything. At dawn, push that little refrigerator of his into his bedroom, so he has food if he needs it when he wakes. Then all you have to do is come out and close the door. It'll lock automatically and it won't open again until sundown."

"Really?"

"It's a vault," Chloe said. "Or a crypt, depending on his mood. Either way, it's how he protects himself during the day. You can do that?"

"Absolutely."

"Okay then. And don't open the street door for anyone, even Garner. At least not until Jude is locked in for the day."

"I can do that."

She watched Chloe leave, then realized she was all alone with Jude. A vampire demon hunter.

Had reality just gotten shot all to hell or what?

The odd thing was, her headache was gone and she felt better than she had in weeks.

Must have to do with having done something really important for a change. It had been a long time since she'd enjoyed that sense of satisfaction.

Jude awoke with a gasp and a jerk, as always. Resurrection carried with it a few uncomfortable seconds. Nor did he get the lazy kind of waking that he'd enjoyed as a human. No. Instant life. Like drawing the first breath out of the womb.

As soon as he had sucked in that first breath, he knew he wasn't alone, and knew who was there. He turned his head and found Terri lying on the bed beside him, her head propped in her hand.

He didn't even bother to ask why she was here. He'd given up asking this woman why she did anything.

"You feel like ice now," she said, running a finger alongside a healing wound on his chest. A quiver of hunger ran through him. "You weren't this cold last night."

"I've been dead all day. It has its effects. Did you enjoy the show?"

She smiled faintly. "I slept a lot. It's not the most amusing show in town. But interesting, anyway."

"How so?"

"Because I'm not quite sure I believed it. Until I put my head to your heart and found it had completely stopped."

"Actually, it beats a few times an hour. Easy to miss. I should feel invaded."

"But you don't?"

He sighed and shook his head. Then he lifted up enough that he could see his chest. The wounds had improved vastly, but the healing was not yet complete. "Damn demons," he muttered and let his head fall back on the pillow.

"Need to feed?" Terri asked.

"Don't tempt me."

"I'm not. I've offered, you've refused. Offer still open. In the meantime, I'll get you a bag if you want."

He wasn't ready yet. "Why did Chloe let you do this?"

"Chloe didn't let me do anything. Well, actually, she left me to make sure you got locked in for the day. She's exhausted, Jude. So I told her I'd take care of things while she went home to shower and sleep. The poor girl needs *some* time."

"Yeah." He sighed and closed his eyes for a moment. The woman's scent was everywhere, maddening, luscious, so exquisite it should have been an expensive perfume. And now it was in his bed, too, and would be there probably stuck in the mattress for weeks, no matter how often he changed sheets.

A good thing he still hurt too much, or he'd have probably rolled over and taken her up on every offer.

She touched him again, just lightly, but it was enough to rouse the Hunger and desire to new heights. He stiffened, fighting impulses so deep in his nature it would take a knife to carve them out. Damn, he wanted her!

"You feel a little warmer now," she remarked, withdrawing her finger.

"Are you through examining me?"

"Sorry." But she didn't exactly look sorry. She looked more curious. "What causes this? How does it happen? Does it change your DNA?"

"How would I know? Do you think I'd turn myself over to a scientist to become a lab specimen?"

"No, I guess not. I'm just curious."

He couldn't blame her for that, he supposed. And he needed to put some space between them. She smelled far too good, and he wasn't exactly feeling strong right now. Somehow that attack last night had left him feeling weak in ways beyond the physical.

Then she crossed the line. *She* did it. He was sure he hadn't invited it, sure he'd been trying to drive her in entirely the opposite direction.

She leaned over before he guessed what she was going to do, and she kissed him on the mouth.

He froze, battling instincts, battling Hunger, battling every sublimated urge of his kind. How could any human ever understand what the warmth of living lips and hands could mean to a vampire?

She pulled away, leaving just a breath of space between them, then leaned in again, kissing him as if she liked the cool sensation of his mouth against hers.

A groan escaped him, and he could not stop himself from lifting his hand, cupping the back of her head, and drawing her deeper to him. Worse, she came willingly, and he felt the drumbeat of his own quickening, wakening blood, felt the pounding of a need he could never explain to anyone who hadn't experienced it. He felt her breast brush his chest, a sensation like lightning.

Desperate, he growled, "Stop. Now." Before he lost it and turned into the kind of monster only one like him could become.

At once she pulled back, her blue eyes wide, her expression somewhere between disappointment and fright.

He pushed up, needing to escape all the possibilities that now hung heavily in the room with them. If she felt frightened, so much the better. What he knew with absolute certainty was that he had to put distance between them *now*.

At least he no longer felt like groaning when he moved, although the wounds still burned like fire, even though they had pretty much closed.

"I'm going to take a shower," he said, making his voice as cold as he could. "It might be a good time for you to step out. I'll unlock the door."

"I'm staying here until you come out of the

shower," she argued. "You still don't look very good."

"I never look good. I'm undead, remember?"

He thought he heard her laugh quietly as he grabbed clothes from his closet, then disappeared into his bathroom. And that laugh, damn it, was as attractive as everything else about her.

The shower was cold, but it hadn't been worth it to him to put in a water heater since temperature had so little effect on him. Although, maybe he should. Terri's remarks about Chloe gave him a pang of conscience. Chloe *did* spend an awful lot of time here during these demonic cases, and surely she deserved a few human comforts. Like a better bed and a hot shower. Maybe even a place to stash clothes.

And then there was Terri. She'd gone from sword-wielding Valkyrie to friend as if someone had flipped a switch. So terrified of him at first, and now...now acting like she was part of his little office family.

Worse, she had kissed him, crossing that

line he'd been so determined to draw. A line he had to put back in place somehow for both their sakes. There was no way she could begin to understand the kind of fire she had just played with, no way he could truly explain it to her.

Could he stand having her around, given how badly he wanted her? Did he have any choice? It was beginning to seem he didn't. The shower got rid of the demon stench, and even some of Terri's lingering perfume. At the rate she was going, that wouldn't last long.

He dressed in the bathroom because he was sure she was still out there, waiting to drive him nuts. Although, to be fair, she probably didn't intend to. Maybe. But how many ways did he have to tell her how much he wanted her, and how dangerous that made him?

Apparently, there weren't enough words in the entire English language.

When he emerged, she was indeed still there, except that she had moved to the chair. He supposed he ought to be grateful for that small mercy.

"What about your job?" he asked.

"I had the day off, but at this point I don't care if I get fired."

He arched a brow but didn't say a word. Now that she was no longer frightened, it seemed that Terri was going to turn into a very interesting package.

They emerged together into the outer office, and Chloe looked up. Then her jaw dropped in astonishment.

"Close your mouth," Jude suggested. "I've been dead all day, remember?"

Chloe promptly shut her mouth, her teeth almost clacking. "Boss, I didn't know…."

Jude managed something approaching a smile. Given how much he still hurt, it was probably more of a grimace. "It's okay. You need your rest, and this one," he said with a jerk of his head toward Terri, "apparently makes her own rules."

"I'm getting that impression."

Terri shrugged. "Sort of like you, Chloe."

Chloe dipped her head, but Terri caught the smile before it could be fully hidden.

"And now," said Jude, "I am drowning in females who constantly disrespect my wishes.

Lovely. Between the two of you and Garner, I'll probably need to be committed before long."

He made his way to the couch and sat, trying not to wince. "Damn demons," he muttered.

"You're spoiled," Chloe said. "The rest of us don't expect to heal overnight from something like that."

"The rest of you aren't vampires." He rubbed his hand over his face. "No hunting tonight."

"No," Terri agreed. "You really don't look good."

Jude frowned at Terri. "Tell me something."

"If I can."

"Why in the world did you follow me last night? I need more than that you felt a compulsion."

She colored faintly, a reaction that had a strong effect on him. Hunger. Desire. This woman was going to drive him insane. "Well, I did feel a compulsion. But I'd been thinking about coming to see you, anyway."

"About what?"

She bit her lower lip, drew a breath, then plunged in. "I've been feeling all week like someone is watching me. Stalking me."

"You think I'm doing that?" The notion annoyed him.

"No." Hastily, she shook her head. "I know you can't be out in the daytime. And anyway...well, frankly, I'm getting to be afraid to go anywhere alone. I won't go out at night anymore unless I absolutely have to. Like last night, I was out only because I have to work late. It's awful, but I don't feel safe anymore."

He frowned. "It might be because of what happened to you last week. A reaction to trauma." Then he vanished into his own thoughts for nearly a minute, turning around possibilities. "Or, it could be that scum Sam. Maybe my suggestion didn't take."

Terri drew a sharp breath. "I haven't seen him. But then, I haven't seen anyone, at least that I've noticed. It's just this creepy feeling. I even have it at work, although not in my apartment, at least not yet. I know it sounds nuts."

He looked from her to Chloe, suddenly certain that he needed to keep an eye on Terri. "Do you want an assistant?" The impulse took him almost by as much surprise as it took Chloe. Too late to snatch the words back though.

Chloe's jaw dropped again. "Really? I'd love some help."

Jude nodded toward Terri. "She seems to cling, and she might be out of a job if she keeps this up."

Chloe looked at Terri. "Easier than trying to break in someone who doesn't begin to know what's going on around here." Then, a wide smile dawned on her face. "That would be cool. Terri?"

"I'd love it. At least for a few hours every night. I still need to keep my day job."

Jude pierced her with his gaze, wishing he could read people's minds. "Why? Why do you want to work here?"

Terri hesitated, biting her lower lip in a way that nearly made Jude groan. That woman had absolutely no idea just how desirable she was in every way. Even that little expression of uncertainty, biting her lip, made him think of the ways he'd like to bite her himself.

"Because," Terri said hesitantly, "it seems like you're doing important stuff. More important than what I do."

"Now that's relative."

Then Jude closed his eyes, letting the pain wash through him, waiting patiently for his body to do its job. Of one thing he was damn sure. He might have just made a very big mistake. Because he had just invited the lamb into his lair.

And she was such a good-smelling lamb.

"Aw, hell," he said suddenly, interrupting the women's conversation. "Would one of you get me a bag? I'm hungrier and wearier than I thought."

"Probably all that healing," Chloe said knowledgeably.

Actually, thought Jude, it was probably Terri. He was going to get well and truly sick of canned blood, trying to leash his hunger.

Just another lash on his journey of atonement, he thought grimly. He deserved every one of them.

And possibly a million more besides.

Chapter 6

Terri found her first night on her new job rather...different. She didn't know exactly how to describe it. Jude, far from being a lion who seemed always on the edge of pouncing, just relaxed. Well, what else could he do?

He was still clearly weakened from his encounter with the demon. He made no pretense of working, just sat on the sofa, sometimes closing his eyes as if another wave of pain washed through him. She wanted to ask why he kept doing this, kept exposing himself to such dangers, but figured she'd get another of his non-answer answers. Or maybe, and possibly worse, she'd hear a truth that would make her unhappy. He seemed to deal out both kinds of responses regularly.

Regardless, with him sitting right there, she couldn't even ask Chloe about him. She did, however, have plenty to learn from Chloe about the job basics: where everything was located, which cases were in active files, where and how they did most of their online research.

And the Rolodex.

The Rolodex fascinated her. Different colored tabs marked the cards.

"The red ones are always to be put directly through to Jude if he's here."

"Important people?"

"Vampires," Chloe said.

Terri blinked. Apparently, she hadn't totally moved past shock. "Uh...there are more?"

Jude spoke almost sarcastically. "I regret, madam, I am not the last of my kind."

"I meant here. In town."

"Yeah, sure, just a couple," Chloe said. "Some of these live elsewhere. Anyway, when they call, it's important. Always."

"Okay. Blue tabs?" There were a half dozen of those.

"Clergy members who help us out." Chloe flipped to one. "This is Father Dan. He helps us most, and he's the only one who really knows what Jude is. The thing is, unless you're talking to him or to one of the red-tabbed cards, watch what you say. You're going to have to learn to cover."

Terri nodded, concealing her surprise that any clergy worked with Jude, and that one apparently knew what he was. She was starting to get used to having her preconceived notions turned on end. "I already did that last night."

"What happened?"

She told Chloe about the neighbor who had complained and what she had said.

"Oh, lovely," Jude drawled from the couch. "Now I'm a dog trainer."

"Did you want me to tell him the truth? My friend the vampire is in there fighting a demon?"

He merely looked sourly at her and said, "It pains me that my assistants have to become such inventive liars."

Chloe sniffed. "I think it pains you more that you were called a dog trainer."

He made a grumpy sound.

Chloe looked at Terri. "I think he's hungry."

"Quit telling me what I am. I'll let you know."

Chloe made a face. "Men don't change at all just because they become vampires. Give them a little demon gash or two and they act like cranky babies."

Terri couldn't help it. She giggled and got a glare from Jude.

"As for the rest of these people," Chloe continued, "the yellow tabs are clients, the green tabs are sources. And none of them, absolutely none of them, knows."

Terri nodded. "I understand."

"We do everything possible to make Jude seem human."

A snort from the direction of the couch.

"When a new client calls, we simply make an appointment for them in the evening, after sunset. We're not exactly overrun with paying clients, so it won't be a big hassle."

Terri was surprised. "Then how do you stay open?"

"I have means," came the answer from the couch. "I haven't been a wastrel for the last two centuries."

"Were you before?"

Jude, who had been leaning back, sat up a little, wincing. "I was the youngest son of the Earl of Kenwick. Which made me absolutely useless."

"How so?"

"Younger sons get no inheritance, no one really wants them about, and my father was prolific to say the least. As his youngest son, I suppose I should be grateful that he bothered to scrape together enough money to purchase my cornetcy in the army. At least I didn't have to go into the church. Although in retrospect…" He let the thought trail off. "Regardless, I never had the opportunity to be a wastrel, unlike my eldest brother. As soon as I came down from Eton, I was in uniform."

"No choices at all?"

"None. One is a product of one's times, after all, and in my times, those were my choices.

Anything else would have shamed my almighty family's honor." An almost-laugh escaped him. "I wish my father could see me now—engaged in business. Trade. Oh, that was a dirty word back then."

"So you were just supposed to be a soldier for the rest of your life?"

"Or marry well. At my station, I could have married my way out of the army, had I the least interest in taking to wife the daughter of some wealthy tradesman who wanted an entrée into society." He gave a shake of his head.

"That's nuts," Chloe said.

"I quite agree. And I think I *am* hungry."

Terri jumped up first and returned quickly with a bag for Jude and a couple of tissues.

"Thank you," he said, the politest words she had heard issue from him in two nights.

"You're welcome."

His eyes studied her for a moment. "You're taking to all of this quite well."

"I'm actually enjoying myself." She returned to her chair beside Chloe, giving him the space from her he seemed to crave. As he drank, more slowly this time, she asked another question.

"So you're a lord?"

He wiped his mouth with a tissue. "No. Never. I was Colonel the Honorable Jude Ashton Messenger. Honorable having to do with my father's status, not my own, I assure you. The military rank I earned."

Terri tried to imagine it, but she knew only the barest history of those times. "It must have been a hard life."

"Better than being in the ranks. Well, except in battle. Someone had to lead. And in those days, officers most assuredly did *not* lead from the rear."

Which, she thought, might explain a great deal about this man.

He took another drink, and wiped his mouth. "I spent a few years in India, then my regiment joined the Peninsular Army in 1809. Served under Wellington all the way through 1814, had a brief furlough, and next thing I knew I was in Belgium. And then…Waterloo."

"I guess I should read some history."

His eyes were lightening again, growing

more golden. "If you want the big picture."
He sighed. "It was a long time ago. So much
of what seemed important to me in my former
life hardly matters anymore. Most especially
to me."

"How are those wounds?"

"They still feel as if someone is holding a
torch to them."

"Ouch," said Chloe. "No better at all?"

"A little. It'll pass." Then he looked at Terri
again. "I felt you praying when you were out
in the hall."

"You could feel that?" The notion amazed
her.

"I wasn't the only one who felt it. I'm sorry
I got so angry with you, Terri, but you have
to promise me to stay away at these times. I
wasn't the only one who sensed you out in the
hall. The demon did, too."

A little chill trickled down her spine. "What
are you trying to say?"

"If I had gotten distracted, it might have
been able to…occupy me. I certainly sensed
it trying to find a way to use you against me.
If you hadn't been praying, I don't know what

might have happened. You cannot, must not, go into these things unprepared. Which is what I keep trying to get through Garner's thick skull."

Chloe put one foot up on her desk. "You know, Jude, maybe it's time you got us all qualified as exorcists."

He sat bolt upright, wincing, but staring at Chloe as if she'd lost her mind. "No. You're safer away."

"Sure, until one of those things follows you home. Garner wants to be involved. Maybe Terri does, too, I don't know." She tightened her lips a bit. "I've been reading, Jude. If one of them follows you back here, we could be in some serious trouble. You at least owe it to us to teach us how to protect ourselves. How to fight if we need to."

Then she pushed back from her desk and stood, stretching. "Well, I'm going to take advantage of having help. I'm outta here. I need some sleep, and for once I'd like to get it at the right time of day. For my kind, anyway. See you tomorrow."

She picked up her purse, smiled a little too brightly, and left.

"Freaking bloody hell," Jude said irritably. "What got into her?" Then he rose and stomped into his office, closing the door.

Leaving Terri all alone in the front office to think about what Chloe had just said. And maybe Chloe was right: maybe they all needed to have at least some idea of how to deal with demons. Remembering what she had faced as a child, what she had been sensing for the last week or so, she shuddered.

But then, almost as if her mind refused to linger on those fears, it skipped to the kiss she had given Jude. Her cheeks colored at the memory, mostly because she couldn't believe her own temerity. She'd never kissed a man first before. She could put it down to overwhelming curiosity, to find out what it was like, whether she would find his lips as cool as his skin, whether she would like it or not.

The thing was, it hadn't been all curiosity. Desire for him seemed to have become an almost subliminal background to her life since he had rescued her. Ridiculous, and according to Jude, dangerous. He kept trying to send her on her way, and she kept coming back.

Until now, she hadn't thought of herself as the kind of person to take unnecessary risks, yet here she was sitting in the office of a vampire. Instead of grabbing her things and leaving, as any sane person would do, she had kissed him, and she shivered with longing every time she remembered him saying, "I want you like hell on fire."

Twenty minutes later, however, Jude opened his office door. "No Garner today?"

"Chloe didn't mention him."

"That's odd." He frowned. "He usually shows up by now."

"Can I call him?"

He raised a brow, then came farther into the office, almost like a man testing the water. If her scent disturbed him so much, maybe he was trying to see how close he could safely get. He wound up back on the couch, as far as he could be from Chloe's desk, where she now sat.

"I need to get you a phone," he remarked.

She pointed to the set on the desk.

"No, I mean a cell phone like mine. I have us all on a special plan that gives us multi-way talk ability, like a radio, but only among ourselves. And given what we deal with around here, I prefer knowing you can all get instantly in touch if you need to regardless of where you are. It only becomes more imperative if someone is indeed stalking you."

"Oh." There didn't seem to be anything else she could say about that. Nor did she want, at the moment, to consider the implications. She was still trying to absorb what had happened last night, what she'd seen and what she'd heard, as well as Jude's warnings. Then there was his apparent acceptance of her feeling of being stalked. Enough to make the back of her neck prickle with fear yet again.

He pulled his own cell out of his pocket, flipped it open and pressed a button. A moment later he said, "So where the hell are you? Why aren't you here annoying me?"

Silence.

Then "Ah. See you then." He snapped the phone closed.

Terri couldn't hide a smile of amusement. "You speak so nicely to him."

"If I give him an inch, he takes a mile. Usually the wrong mile."

"Is he coming?"

"Later. Seems he has a hot date."

"Lucky him."

All of a sudden the air in the room seemed as thick as syrup. As if everything had slipped into slow motion, and breathing became difficult. She was alone with Jude. A vampire she had dared to kiss in hopes of discovering that she wouldn't like it. Instead, she had found she liked it a lot. Alone with a vampire who said he wanted her like hell on fire.

The worst of it was, she began to feel the same way. Her heart skipped, then started a slow, steady beating. She couldn't look away from his golden eyes.

"I can hear your heart," he told her. "It gives away your secrets."

She swallowed. "Really?"

"You don't even know what it is you think you want."

"Yes, I do."

"No, you don't. Because what you want is something you know nothing about. It's not in the library of your experience. And be honest with yourself, Terri. You're not even really sure it's what you want. You're tempted, you're curious, you feel drawn. But you're afraid, too."

It was true. She managed to tear her gaze from his and look down at the desk. "Would you be happier if I just left? Permanently?"

"A week ago I said so, didn't I?"

Her heart slammed and her stomach sank. "Then I'll go."

"No. Oddly…I seem to have changed my mind on that. I can handle the temptation. Just quit…inviting me."

Lifting her eyes again, she looked at him. "How so?"

"Everything about you. The way you look at me. The way you move. Even that kiss you gave me, however tentative you tried to be. You're attracted and it shows in a million ways." Then he gave a short, sharp laugh. "Forget it. It's like asking you to change the way you breathe, and the way you breathe is tempting enough." He waved a hand. "I'll manage. But do you even know why you keep coming back? Is it just fascination?"

"I don't think so." She hesitated. "That's probably part of it. But there's also a compulsion of some kind. I knew, just knew, I had to be there last night, Jude. I was screaming at myself to stop, but something *else* made me go up there and stay even when I guessed what was going on. I don't know what it is, but after last night, standing in that hallway scared half to death and praying as hard as I could, I can tell you it's not fascination."

"Now *I'm* fascinated," he remarked quietly. "And not just because you're the most tempting human morsel to cross my path in at least a couple of lifetimes. A compulsion." He frowned faintly. "I wonder if you have some kind of Gift."

"Gift?"

"Like Garner. He senses demonic presences, infestations. It's like he was born with a radar for the minions of hell."

"Oh." She tried to conceive of it and failed. Nor could she imagine what kind of gift she might have. "I don't know, Jude. Except for living in a haunted house when I was a kid, my life has been perfectly ordinary."

"Haunted house?" His brows lifted, then knit in thought. "I want to talk about that, but later. First we have some other things to do."

"Like what?"

He rose. "I'm getting my coat. It's not very late yet. Let's go get you a cell phone and a few other things."

"What other things?"

He smiled. "If you're going to work with me, Terri, you need to carry holy water and a cross at all times—or whatever your particular preferred religious symbol is. Still want the job?"

Something deep inside her answered before her brain could. "Yes."

"Then let's go."

Evidently, Jude had more than one long black leather coat. He emerged from his office wearing a fresh one, and filled the pockets with the items still lying on Chloe's desk from last night.

"I'm still not very strong," he remarked after

they climbed into the car. "Which means I can't offer you a full measure of protection. So if I tell you to do something, just do it. Promise me."

"I promise." She wondered what he was worried about. Or maybe he was just making a general statement.

She learned something at the cell phone store, though. Even though there were quite a few customers, and every sales person seemed to be engaged, the instant Jude's eyes settled on one, he excused himself from the person he was talking to and hurried over.

"I want to add Dr. Black to my business plan and get her a phone."

The guy practically tripped over his words. "Yes, sir. Immediately, sir. Let's go to the computer and see what we have."

Jude smiled faintly and walked over toward the desk, the sea parting before him as people glanced his way, then edged back. They didn't seem consciously disturbed, but they created a hole around him.

Terri was amused. The salesman continued too eagerly, racing through the phone selection and updating the account. As if he couldn't wait to be done with the transaction. In an amazingly short space of time, they were out the door, Terri with a new phone in hand.

"I can see one advantage to being a vampire," Terri remarked as they drove away.

"Which is?"

"If I'd walked into that store alone they probably wouldn't have gotten to me before closing time."

Jude chuckled, but quietly, as if it hurt. "I do have a way of getting attention when I want it."

"And when you don't?"

"Easy enough to blend with shadows."

Twenty minutes later, they pulled up in front of a steepled brick church. Lightning flickered silently overhead as Jude gathered up some plastic bottles from his backseat. Then they walked to the entrance where Jude pulled out his key ring and unlocked the front door of the church. When they stepped inside, the only light came from a red sanctuary lamp near the front of the church.

When he had closed the door, she heard him
lock it behind them. Only then did he flip a
switch and turn on some dim lights.

"It's a beautiful church," Terri breathed ap-
preciatively. As lightning flickered, she noticed tall stained-glass windows running along
either side of the rows of pews.

"Not a very busy one anymore," Jude remarked. "But yes, it's beautiful. Built at a time
when a concrete box wasn't considered to be
the height of architectural expression. Let's get
these bottles filled. The font is right over here."

Terri stood beside him, handing him one
bottle after another as he filled them.

"A spray bottle?" That definitely surprised
her.

"Maximum coverage, minimum wastage,"
he said. "Actually quite efficient in a pinch.
Let's go sit for a minute."

She followed him up the aisle to the rear
pew and sat beside him. He reached in his
pocket, and this time he pulled out a necklace.
It caught the light enough that she could see it
was a cross.

"Not very pretty," he remarked. "But this is

all I have that's already blessed. I'll get you a nicer one."

"It doesn't matter what it looks like," she said impulsively. "That's not what's important, is it?"

He smiled, and for him it was a strangely soft smile. "No, that's not what's important. And you must be the first woman I've ever known to turn down the offer of a better piece of jewelry."

"Then you know the wrong women."

Her heart fluttered a bit as he opened the clasp of the necklace, then leaned forward to put it around her neck. The touch of his fingers as he fastened it was cool and erotic. A shiver ran through her, and her heart speeded a bit.

"Tut," he said, but he was still smiling. "And in a church."

"Sorry."

His hands, instead of sliding away immediately, cupped her cheeks gently. Oh so gently, a cool touch that felt good in ways she couldn't begin to describe. "Don't apologize. I was just teasing."

His hands lingered, and even in the dim

light she could see his eyes darken. Then, as he had once before, he leaned close enough to inhale her scent. She felt the tension grip him, waited almost frozen herself, acutely aware that he could, if he wanted, take her blood then and there. And that he wanted to. That he had a hunger for her beyond mere desire, one she couldn't begin to understand.

He released her, and disappointment filled her. She wanted that touch again. More of it. Much more of it. She had to bite her lip to keep from saying so.

"I have a St. Michael medal for you when we get back to the office. Pin it inside your clothing, okay?"

"Okay." She looked down at the bottles of holy water sitting between them as her fingers touched the cross on the necklace he had put on her. All of reality seemed to be shifting beneath her feet, carrying her ever deeper into the very world that had so terrified her as a child.

Did she really want to face this? Deep down, she felt as if she had refused to truly face these issues once before. Yes, she had fought back, and successfully, but then she had banished the incident from her thoughts without ever trying to understand what had happened. Without dealing with what it might have meant.

She looked at him again, still fingering the cross. "These things really work?"

"If there's evil, and there is, don't you think there must be good forces to counter it?"

"But these are just objects."

"And objects, because of faith, have powers." He turned and faced the front of the church. "What do you know about voodoo dolls?"

"Probably the little that most people know."

"When they're created, their maker infuses them with power. The power of belief. And I can assure you, Terri, they work whether the recipient believes it or not. The same with that cross, and the holy water. They're infused with power because they were blessed as an act of faith. Faith infused them. Your faith, if you can find it, will make them even stronger."

"I have faith. You heard me praying last night."

"True."

"Why do you have a key to the church? So you can get holy water?"

"Not just that. I have keys to a few churches. Sometimes the only sanctuary is holy ground."

That caused a shiver to trickle down her spine. "You mean you sometimes have to hide here?"

"It happens. Not often, but it happens."

He sat staring toward the altar for a little longer, then sighed. "Time to head back. I've been out of touch too long, and Garner should be arriving soon."

Terri doubted it, not if Garner had a hot date, but she didn't argue.

She watched Jude genuflect and followed suit.

What a complex man he was, full of seeming contradictions.

But then she wondered where those contradictions really came from. Were they an artifact of what she'd always believed about vampires? Or was Jude just a huge exception?

And she wondered if she would ever know.

Chapter 7

Garner still hadn't arrived when they returned to the office. Terri slipped into a small room that held a cot, probably for Chloe, and followed Jude's instructions to pin the St. Michael medal on the inside of her clothing. A glance in the mirror of the powder room told her that the cross he had given her must be stainless steel. Plain, ordinary, and, if Jude was right, very powerful. She touched it, decided it looked okay, and returned to the office.

Jude once again sat on the couch.

"How are you feeling?" she asked him as she took up position at the desk.

"Better, actually. The burning has begun to subside."

"Good."

"Now I want something."

"Blood?"

He shook his head. "No, I'm fine. What I want is information. About you."

"Oh." She hesitated. "I don't talk much about myself."

"I've noticed. Why not?"

"I'm not a very exciting person. I have more fun listening to other people than talking."

"I think you're a very exciting person," he said, and something in his gaze made her heart speed up again, and that made him smile, because he could hear it.

"The haunting," he said. "Tell me about that haunting you mentioned."

"Other than that it was scary?" When he nodded, she tried to decide where to begin. "I noticed it the first night we moved into a new house. I was five at the time, and I honestly didn't know what to make of it. It wasn't as if I saw anything, or heard anything. It was just this feeling that someone was always there, watching me. And I didn't like it but I couldn't figure out how to express the feeling. It wasn't as if I could say someone was there because obviously no one was."

"Very difficult experience at that age."

"For a long time, that's all it was. But night after night I'd lie in my bed with my eyes wide open, just waiting, sure I was going to see something sooner or later. I refused to sleep in the dark. Some nights, when the feeling got too strong, I'd try to hide myself under the covers, as if I could make myself invisible to it."

He nodded encouragingly.

"The feeling never went away, but at some point I convinced myself it wasn't real. I got better at living with it, even ignoring it."

"Why do I suspect it didn't end there?"

"It didn't. I heard it the first time when I was about eight. It called my name. Just this quiet whisper in the dark. So it was back to sleeping with the lights on, even though my parents got angry with me about it. And I told them I heard someone calling my name. They put it down to overactive imagination."

Her hands clenched, because now she was

getting to the part that still terrified her, even after all this time. "Things started happening fast after that. I began to see shadows out of the corner of my eye, but when I looked they were gone. And if ever I was alone in a room, I'd hear it whisper my name. Then it started moving things in my room. The worst night was when it pulled my blankets off me."

"So it was definitely interested in you. No one else heard or saw anything?"

She shook her head. "They just kept telling me I was dreaming it, I was being difficult, even wondering if I needed to see a psychologist. But then…I actually saw it. Saw the black shadow of a man in the corner of my room, even though the lights were on. I finally told my best friend about it, because I was so scared. Amazingly, she didn't laugh at me. She gave me a holy card, told me what prayers to say. I did it and the thing went away."

"That must have been a relief."

She laughed with little humor. "At first. But then I spent a long time worrying it might turn up again."

"Did it?"

"It didn't, and eventually I got past it."

He appeared thoughtful, but in a way that speeded her pulse. His gaze was so intent, and could be so intense when he looked at her. "So sure you got rid of it," he said, more to himself than to her. Then, "What you experienced was what we in the business call infestation."

Her head jerked back and a sense of creeping horror began to fill her. "Demons?"

"We're not quite clear on that. What we are clear on is that some people seem to be more susceptible to such things than others. What compelled you to follow me last night? What do you feel watching you? And certainly last night you were noticed. Most definitely noticed."

"By the demon?"

"Yes. Maybe your experience in childhood marked you in some way. These things are always looking for a doorway to wedge themselves through. Maybe your childhood experience marked you as an opening."

The thought horrified even more than discovering Jude was a vampire. "You mean it might be starting again?"

"I don't know. But for argument's sake, let's say you're marked. Let's say you were compelled to follow me by something outside yourself."

"But how could that possibly be?"

He frowned. "It happens occasionally. When an exorcism is about to be performed, the possessing demon will try to draw someone susceptible close enough so it can change hosts easily."

"Oh, my God." She felt almost physically ill. "Oh, my God. What do I do?"

"Nothing at the moment. Clearly, though, I need to keep an eye on you." He was frowning again, obviously thinking, and whatever he was thinking he chose not to share. Given that Jude was an extraordinarily blunt man most of the time, that troubled her deeply.

Out of the blue, he asked, "Otherwise?"

"Otherwise? You mean the rest of my life? Average. I had friends, I dated occasionally. Well, average except I went to college at sixteen and medical school at nineteen."

"No mad, torrid romances?"

She shook her head. "Not really."

"Hmm."

"Hmm?"

"As lovely as you are, I find that surprising. I would have expected something quite different."

"I just haven't met the right person, I guess." Then she admitted, "Something always goes wrong."

"In what way?"

"Well, it's not just one way. I'll date someone, and then after a few dates he'll say or do something that makes me feel, I don't know, as if I'm not all that important."

"You do apologize a lot."

"If you'd grown up with my mother, you'd know why. I was almost always wrong."

"Or at least she thought so. And yet I see quite a bit of spunk in you, so she didn't manage to quash you."

"I guess not."

"Well, I'd like you to stop apologizing to me all the time. Especially when it's about who you are. Yes, your scent maddens me, but that's not something you should apologize for. It's not as if you choose to drive me crazy, unlike Garner, for example."

One corner of her mouth lifted. "Are you sure he's trying?"

"Sometimes I definitely think so. Other times…" He shrugged. "Perhaps not so much. He *does* worry me, though."

Jude, she had noticed, really cared about those who worked with him. Those he had let into his inner circle and his secrets. His frustration with Garner seemed to her to be born more out of concern for the young man getting himself into trouble than from anything else.

She spoke. "You feel a strong sense of *noblesse oblige,* don't you?"

He arched a brow. "I don't care for that term. It implies I'm somehow above and others are somehow below me in station. I don't see it that way at all. One cares for people because one cares. Because they deserve it."

"Maybe so. But I still feel as if you put an umbrella of protection over everyone in this office."

"Only because I can. When I can. And since

I miss nearly half of every day, there are big gaps in that umbrella, as you call it."

She hesitated, wondering if she might anger him, but then asked the question anyway. "Is the night so awful?"

"Actually, it's quite beautiful. I have senses you can't imagine, so even the darkest night is full of color, the quietest, full of sound. I can, quite literally, hear the grass grow. I can hear the musical sounds as a tree sucks water up its trunk. I can hear the heartbeat of a sleeping baby through walls and from a huge distance. I hear the night murmurs of dreamers I can't even see, the sounds of love being played out in privacy."

"Doesn't it overwhelm you?"

"I can choose to filter it out. The same way you do with a lot of things."

"That must be incredible." She tried, but failed, to even imagine it.

"It is. Sometimes I take it for granted, but others I simply swim in it. I drink it in and revel in it."

She saw him start to rise, and the next instant he was standing beside her, over her.

"Don't move," he murmured. "Not even a little."

She looked up at him from her chair, saw the golden eyes staring down at her. Her heart almost skittered to a stop. He was a predator, and right now she believed it to her very bones.

She froze, instinct taking over.

Then he leaned toward her, slowly, as if he didn't want to frighten her. "Don't move," he whispered.

She didn't think she could have, at that moment. Was he about to drink from her?

His hands cupped her cheeks, cool and smooth, smoother than human flesh. He touched her mouth with his. A light touch. His lips were parted, and he inhaled, taking her breath into him. He sighed, and she felt the coolness of his breath like an autumn breeze.

Then he kissed her. Lightly. Gently. Almost worshipfully.

And that touch, that lightest, gentlest of touches, crackled and popped throughout her like lightning. She wanted him. She wanted him here, now, in whatever way he wanted to take her. On the desk, on the floor, she didn't care. Desire pounded in her like a jack-hammer.

Mindlessly, she leaned into that kiss, and started to raise her arms, needing him closer, heedless of risk.

And then he was gone.

She opened her eyes, blinking, startled and disappointed, and found he had withdrawn to the couch.

"I moved," she said, understanding.

"Well, yes, that does make it a bit harder to hang on to my self-control." But then he smiled. "It was worth it."

For some darn reason, as disappointed as she felt, she smiled right back at him. "That was amazing."

"Which is one very good reason it would be nice if Garner would show up. While I'm not opposed to giving you what you want, especially since I want it myself, I'm not at all sure you're ready, or that you won't regret it."

"That's a decision for me, isn't it?"

His eyes darkened visibly. "There you go, tempting me again."

"I don't get it, Jude."

"Which is exactly the problem. I could have you naked in my bed before you catch your next breath. In fact, it's all I can do to refuse what you offer so sweetly. With others, I wouldn't even hesitate."

"Then what's wrong with me?"

"Nothing," he answered flatly. "Absolutely nothing. It's me. I don't want to do something that might eventually make you hate me. And it could, Terri. It could. With you, I'm wary of my own selfishness. I don't want you to wake up some morning full of disgust and self-loathing because you gave yourself to an undead bloodsucker."

She gasped. "Don't talk about yourself that way!"

"Why not? It's true. I'm not human anymore. That means a whole lot of things that could eventually cause you pain. While I'm an undead bloodsucker, I still have a conscience. And apparently a soul, if Father Dan is to be believed. I've sullied it enough. I sure as hell am not going to sully you."

It pained her to admit he might be right. She was racing into this like a child with no awareness of all the possible dangers. In the process of doing so, she was making his life more difficult, too.

She sighed. "I guess you're right. So it's never?"

He didn't answer for several long seconds. "I didn't say that," he said finally. "But…I need you to better understand what I am, what this would mean. And I need you to be around long enough that I can be reasonably certain you're not just reacting to fascination and curiosity as much as anything. Then…perhaps."

He surprised her with a crooked smile. "We haven't even had a first date yet. How can you be sure I won't disappoint you by the third?"

She managed a laugh, more for his benefit than anything. He was absolutely right, of course. But that didn't ease the hunger that danced through her body like a witch's spell. If he wanted her like hell on fire, it seemed she wanted him just as much.

And she had never, ever, in her life wanted anything as much as she wanted this.

"I'll behave," she said. "At least I'll try."

"I'll try, too." Again he paused. "I don't

know if I can explain this. But your scent... the instant I smelled it the night I found you, I knew it was special. I knew that at one time I would have followed it around the globe if necessary. I would have hunted you to the ends of the earth no matter how far you fled."

"Oh," she breathed. A thrill ran through her but she honestly couldn't have said whether it was a good one or a bad one.

At that moment, the phone rang, rescuing her from the direction her thoughts wanted to take. She glanced at Jude and he nodded, so she lifted the receiver.

"Messenger Investigations. This is Terri. May I help you?"

Chloe's excited voice answered her. "Terri... Terri, is Jude there? I need to talk to him right now."

"Just a second." She held the receiver out toward Jude. "It's Chloe."

He rose and came over to take it. "What's up?"

He listened for a minute, then said, "No, you don't have to come in. I'm sure Terri and I can research it. Just get your rest. All right. Good night."

He hung up and looked at Terri. "There was a savage rape in the warehouse district last night."

Terri's heart almost stopped. "Like the one you saved me from?"

"Possibly. Chloe evidently thinks so. She said the media are reporting four attackers were involved." His face had hardened, and his eyes had changed in some way. Darkening, though not turning black.

"We need to do some research. I need the police report."

"How do we get that?"

"Move aside and I'll show you."

She vacated Chloe's chair and let him sit in front of the computer.

As it happened, he didn't show her anything. His fingers flew over the keys too fast for her to see, maybe at the very edge of whatever speed limited the computer's ability to take in the data.

Then an image of a typed police report appeared on the screen. "How can you access that?" she whispered.

"Detective Matthews showed me how, although I'm sure she doesn't remember."

Terri bit her lip, holding back a protest about legalities. What was the point? Jude could probably walk into the precinct and simply ask for a copy. She was learning that people always did what Jude wanted. Like that clerk at the phone store. Another one of the mysteries that surrounded him.

The image of the report vanished from the screen almost as soon as it appeared. Apparently, he not only moved faster than a human, he read faster, too.

"It sounds like the same crew," he said grimly.

She swallowed. "The…victim?"

"In the hospital. Badly injured, but not so badly she couldn't give a description of the attackers. She's alive because a night watchman heard the fracas and shot over their heads."

"Oh, my God." Terri felt sickened, for the victim, and for what might have happened to her except for Jude.

Jude touched her arm, lightly and briefly. "Sit," he said almost gently. "You look ghastly."

She found a chair beside the desk and dropped onto it like stone. "They've got to be stopped."

"I know."

Something in his voice made her look at him. His eyes had gone black as night again, and something in the set of his face made her shudder. "Jude, there are four of them. I don't care how fast or how powerful you may be, there are still four of them. You can't go after them alone."

"Did I say I would?"

"I don't know why you should have to go after them at all. The police can deal with this."

His gaze grew distant, as if he were searching something just beyond sight. "I smelled something that night."

"The night you saved me?"

He gave a short nod. Then his gaze snapped back to her. "I'm in no condition to do anything tonight, anyway. But I need more information."

"What did you smell?"

"That's just it," he said tightly. "I didn't recognize it." Then he shoved his hand into his pocket and pulled out his cell phone.

"How's that hot date going?" he asked without preamble.

Silence.

"Sorry you didn't score," he said, his voice dripping with sarcasm. "Generally speaking, women don't like men who think of them as scores on a tote board, even if the stupid male isn't stupid enough to say it aloud."

Another silence, Jude looking more impatient by the second. "Garner, I don't give a damn about your damaged ego. We've got a problem and I need you. *Now.*"

He snapped the phone closed and tucked it back into his pocket. "Now we'll find out if that idiot is worth all the trouble he causes me."

Terri, who had listened to the conversation with her jaw steadily dropping in amazement, managed to ask, "What are you going to do?"

"Put him to work. He's been begging

for it, now he'll get it. And we'll find out if he's worth as much salt as he seems to think he is."

She paused, trying to think of a sensible thing to say, but given all that she didn't yet understand, the only thing that came to mind was "He *really* thinks of women as scores?"

Jude tipped his head back, looking at the ceiling. "*I* wasn't the one who first used the word." Then he gave Terri an almost grim smile. "There's a lot we need to teach that boy. A lot."

She decided she rather liked the way he included her in that *we.* "What do you want me to do?"

He started to answer when the front doorbell rang. "Garner couldn't possibly have gotten here that fast," Jude muttered. He punched a button on the computer and suddenly there was a CCTV image filling the screen.

And Jude started to smile. "Terri?"

"Yes?"

"Can you handle being in the room with *two* vampires?"

* * *

The new arrival was a handsome auburn-haired man, slightly taller than Jude, who appeared to be in his mid-thirties. He, too, seemed to prefer to dress in black—probably, Terri thought, because it would make him harder to see in the shadows.

One thing relieved her right off the bat: she didn't feel attracted to him. So that meant her attraction to Jude wasn't merely some vampire-induced fascination. Although she had to admit that being attracted to any vampire at all would just a short time ago have struck her as borderline lunacy.

"Terri," Jude said, "this is an old friend of mine, Creed Preston. Creed, meet Dr. Black. She works with me."

Creed Preston, his eyes nearly as dark as Jude's, hesitated momentarily, then gave her a small bow. "She knows?"

"Yes."

"My." Creed's dark eyes came back to Terri, seeming to pierce her with their curiosity. "You take so many risks, Jude."

"No more than I need to."

Terri had to fight an instinctive urge to back away, impossible given that she was sitting in a chair, but then Creed released her and turned his attention back to Jude.

She spoke. "So, um, how many centuries have you two known each other?"

There was a moment of frozen silence, then Creed laughed and finally gave her a smile. "Only one," he acknowledged.

"So what brings you here?" Jude asked.

"My granddaughter."

Astonishment caused Terri to speak. "You mean you guys can have kids?" The thought of vampire two-year-olds was a little much, and the image that sprang to her mind wasn't pretty.

"No," Jude answered. "We can't."

"Oh."

Creed regarded Terri for a moment. "I gather she doesn't know all that much about us."

"She's learning. What's up with your granddaughter?"

"She's in the hospital. You heard about that attack last night?"

Jude's brows lifted as he looked at his friend. "That was your granddaughter?"

"Yes." Creed almost hissed the word. "I visited her tonight at the hospital and there's an odor to her wounds. Something...unnatural. Since you've made the unnatural your business, I was going to ask you to help me hunt these bastards down. They're going to pay for this."

Jude nodded gravely. "We're getting ready to hunt them. Terri here was almost attacked by them, too. At least we think they're the same ones."

"Then come with me now."

"I can't."

"Why the hell not?"

"Because I was attacked by a demon last night. I'm still not in any condition to hunt. But I've got someone on his way right now who can help locate these scum."

Creed frowned, but finally he nodded. "If that's the best you can do, then all right."

"For tonight," Jude reassured him. "Just for tonight. I'm nowhere near back to full strength, but I promise you, we'll get them."

"Not without me," Creed said darkly.

Terri shivered at his tone. It carried death.

"Not without you," Jude promised. "But don't try it on your own, either. There's something about these guys, and if you try to take on four men who are under unnatural control, you're going to need help."

"Damn." Creed whirled almost too fast to see, then came to light on the edge of the sofa. "Do you have any idea what they did to her?"

"I read the police report."

Creed's hands bunched as if they wanted to close around someone's throat. "She's barely alive, Jude. Barely."

"You could…"

"No!" Creed snapped. "Not that. I want her to have a normal life, not this…*this*…" He left the sentence incomplete, but Terri could not mistake his revulsion. Did all vampires hate themselves? But now was not the time to ask.

"I understand," Jude said. But before he could say more, the bell rang again and Garner's face appeared on the screen.

"There he is," Jude said. He leaned over to press the door release. Moments later, Garner sauntered into the room, trying very hard to look like a young man who had not suffered a major disappointment just a little while ago.

When he saw Creed, he stopped dead in the doorway. "Another one?"

Creed just shook his head and rolled his eyes.

"Jeez, just asking," Garner said, before turning to Jude. "What do you want me to do?"

"Creed here is a good friend of mine, Garner. Got it?"

The young man nodded eagerly. "Got it. And?"

"And you're going to go with him."

Garner paled a bit. "Jude, man, I know *you're* okay, but…*him?*"

"He's not going to hurt you. But he needs your help. I thought you wanted to help, Garner."

"I do, but…" He eyed Creed warily.

Creed sighed impatiently. "Forget it, Jude. I don't need some frightened pantywaist to help me."

"Hey," Garner protested. "I'm no…whatever that is!"

Creed looked dubious beyond words.

"Creed," Jude said, "I know you're upset. But Garner has a Gift."

One of Creed's brows lifted. "What kind?"

"He's got a nose for the unnatural. A good one."

Garner actually puffed a bit. "I do," he said firmly.

Jude's glance silenced any further bragging. "So here's how it's going to be. Are you listening, Garner?"

"Yeah, man."

"Okay. Creed is going to take you to the hospital. His granddaughter was attacked by those same thugs who tried to attack Terri."

"You guys can have grandkids? No way."

Jude snorted impatiently. "Yes, way. Are you listening?"

Garner nodded quickly.

"They smelled odd to me. Creed smelled something unnatural about his granddaughter's wounds. So he's going to take you to the hospital. Memorize the scent. Identify it if you can. Then the two of you are going to take a walk around the warehouse district and see if you can figure out where those thugs are."

"At *night?*" Garner almost squeaked. "I'm not going down there at night."

"Garner." Jude's voice became hard, commanding. "You're going under the protection of a vampire. It doesn't matter that it's night. But we've got to find those thugs before they do this again. Got it?"

Garner glanced at Creed, swallowed, then nodded. "Okay, Jude."

"You wanted to be part of this. Here's your chance. But listen to me. I do not want either of you mixing with these guys. Not when there's four of them. Just find them, if you can, and come back here."

"Okay," Garner said. "Okay. I can do that."

"See that you do exactly that and no more. Creed?"

The other vampire stood, looking drawn but strong. "I said I wouldn't do anything, didn't I?"

"Just make sure nothing happens to Garner. He's only a human."

"I noticed." Sarcastic.

Then the odd couple walked out the door, Garner tossing suspicious glances at Creed with every step, leaving Terri and Jude alone once again.

That's when Terri noticed that Jude had begun to look paler than usual. Almost gray. "What's wrong?" she asked, leaping to her feet. "Those wounds?"

"I'll be fine. It's that damned canned blood. It takes longer to heal."

He went to the couch and sat, grimacing. "I should be out there with Creed and Garner."

"Not in this condition." She went to sit beside him. "Besides, Creed promised he wouldn't do anything on his own, so they should be safe. You don't need to worry."

Dark eyes, eyes that now seemed darker than the night itself, looked at her. "If it were my granddaughter lying in that hospital bed, and I found those thugs, I'd probably break every law, every rule I've made for myself and every promise I'd given anyone. Do you think I wouldn't?"

She saw the truth in his eyes. Felt it shudder through her. Honestly, she couldn't blame him.

She'd seen cases in her own professional life that had horrified her enough that she might have taken the law into her own hands.

"What do you mean by unnatural?" she asked finally, seeking at least to push the thoughts of him killing into the background. "If it's a demon, wouldn't you recognize the smell?"

"Sometimes. First, I don't have Garner's Gift. Second, there are different kinds of demons. Levels, types…oh, there's a multitude of evil beings out there. A whole damn pantheon. Unless I've met a particular kind before, I can't identify it, beyond its being unnatural."

"Lovely." Also terrifying. She thought about her feeling of being watched and realized she didn't feel it here with Jude. What did that mean?

As she kept watching him, she felt deep concern rising. He really didn't look good at all. She drew a steadying breath and asked, "Would fresh blood help you?"

The look he gave her spoke volumes, about hunger, about lust, about things she couldn't begin to imagine. Then he tore his gaze away. "Forget it," he said shortly.

"Forget it? When you're suffering? I don't think so."

"I'd have to go out to get fresh. Not tonight. I need to be here in case they find something."

"You don't have to go out to get fresh."

He became absolutely, positively still, a statue carved from black-and-white marble. After a moment he said, "Terri, no."

"Jude, yes." Impulsively, she reached out and took his hand. He made a halfhearted attempt to pull it away, then quit trying when her fingers tightened. "I'd give a transfusion to a patient in the hospital. Do you think I'd do any less for you when you saved my life? I might be the one lying in the hospital bed right now like Creed's granddaughter."

"Don't tempt me."

"I'm not tempting. I'm offering." She pulled the collar of her blouse away from her neck. "Take what you need."

"You don't know what I need."

"You said it would be less than a blood donation."

"You don't understand!"

"How can I if you don't tell me? And right now you need blood. Fresh blood you said. I know for a fact that I can spare over seven hundred milliliters without even noticing. So take a pint. A half-pint. Whatever it is you need because I'm not going to just accept doing nothing when I can help you!"

His gaze had fastened on her throat, and there was a tension she had never before seen in his face. Was that how a tiger looked before it sprang? Her mouth turned dry.

But the doctor in her wouldn't let it go. Nor would, if she were to be honest, the woman in her. Whatever had made this man so central to her life, so quickly, she couldn't ignore it. She couldn't just stand by.

"Not the throat." He spoke in a near growl.

"Why not?"

"You wouldn't be able to hide it. You'd have to explain. Anyway, it's too intimate." He closed his eyes, murmuring, "God forgive me."

"For what?" A frisson of panic fluttered through her. "What are you going to do?"

His eyes opened, blacker than death. "I'm going to drink from you."

"Okay." Her voice quavered a little. "Do I need to know anything? To get prepared?"

He drew a long, deep breath. "I'm going to lick you. My saliva will numb you, so you don't feel the puncture."

She managed a jerky nod. "Where?"

His expression shifted, going from frightening to almost dreamy, and somehow that eased her apprehension.

"I could bite you anywhere," he murmured. "But for now…"

He pulled the collar of her shirt over her shoulder, then he tugged her bra strap out of the way. Slowly, caressingly, his cool fingertips brushed back and forth beneath her collar bone, above her breast. A shiver of mixed delight and fear raced through her. "Somewhere here," he whispered. "There's a vein…" His fingers paused. "Here."

He could feel a vein that easily? But before she had time to feel fully amazed, his head swooped toward her. She felt the brush of his cool tongue over her skin, and a ripple of astonishing pleasure passed through her.

Then...

For an instant, nothing. She looked down at the top of his dark head, and wondered when he would do it.

But all of a sudden, as if a switch were flipped, she felt the oddest sensation. Her own heartbeat seemed to grow loud in her ears, her thoughts drifted away on a tide of bliss, and her body began to throb with intense pleasure, in time to her heart.

Dimly she realized what he had meant about giving her a sexual thrill. It was a thrill her wildest imaginings would never have even suggested to her.

Even those thoughts drifted away. Hardly aware of doing it, she raised a hand and cupped the back of his head, holding him to her, giving him her life willingly.

She existed now in timeless moments of feeling. Good feelings. Sexual feelings that nearly made her moan, but something even more. Something at least as deep and satisfying, but unlike any experience she had ever had.

Her head fell back as she cradled him to her and gave herself up to the most intense, arousing experience she had ever had. She wanted it to never end.

Slowly, reluctantly, she grew aware again. Felt his cool tongue lap at her skin. Gently. Almost adoringly.

All too soon, he lifted his head and looked at her.

Her eyelids drooped and she saw him through her lashes. His gaze was golden now, more vigorous than she had seen it since the attack. He licked his lips, wiping away traces of her blood, then leaned forward and kissed her on the mouth.

This was no tentative kiss. This was a deep, demanding kiss, one that almost seemed to claim her. Her body leapt again in response, and she wrapped her arms around him, tilting her head to take his tongue even deeper into her. Oh, how she wanted him, in every way possible.

Then, too quickly to observe or absorb, he

was gone. Her arms were empty, her body screaming for more.

She blinked and found him at the far end of the couch.

"Thank you," he said.

She struggled to find her emotional footing, to ground herself once again in the familiar reality. It wasn't easy, because he had carried her to a world she had never guessed existed.

She wanted to reach for him again, but stopped because she noted that something was different in the way he looked at her. Something almost wary.

She fought for her voice and found it. "Did you get enough?"

He nodded, never taking those watchful eyes from her.

"Did I do something wrong?"

A harsh laughed escaped him. "No. But I almost did."

Confusion. Her head whirled a moment, then steadied. "What do you mean?"

"Another time," he answered obliquely. Then he sprang from the couch, again almost too fast to see, and began to pace the office. "It's working. Thank you."

"You feel better?"

"More than I can tell you. My strength is returning." He faced her then. "I need to go out and look for Garner and Creed. Help them."

Terri jumped up. "Not without me."

"Terri, you can't do this. You don't have any special skills."

"How do you know that? I fought off a demon, didn't I? All on my own. And I've got a personal interest in catching those thugs."

He glared at her. She glared back.

"Your blood pressure is too low," he argued.

"Don't try to lie to me, Jude. I don't feel in the least light-headed. My heart isn't racing. You didn't even take a full pint, and you could have taken more."

"What about work?" he demanded. "You have to go to the office in the morning."

"I have three days off."

"Woman, you've been a thorn in my side from the outset."

"Good. From what I can see, you need a few more."

His face creased. "What in the world are you talking about?"

"You don't listen to Chloe at all, and she's probably one of the best friends you've got. You just sent Garner, of all people, out to hunt those thugs with no protection except a vampire neither of us trust not to try to take them out himself."

"Creed promised."

"And his promise won't be worth a hill of beans if he finds his granddaughter's attackers. You said it yourself, Jude. But you sent Garner because you felt weak and couldn't go with Creed yourself. And you knew that if he walked out of here alone he would do it himself."

Jude scowled at her. For some reason the expression no longer terrified her.

"What's more," she added in the coup de grace, "you only took my blood because you're afraid that if you don't get out there Creed will do something stupid."

"Back when I was human," he said, "women used to listen to a man."

"Back when you were human they just manipulated you more subtly."

He continued to glare at her, but not for long. A sigh escaped him, almost a laugh but not quite. "Damn women," he muttered.

"Damn vampires," she retorted.

Five minutes later, once he was sure she was properly armed with holy water as well as her cross and her St. Michael's medal, they headed out together.

Chapter 8

Jude considered the all-too-few ways he could kill himself, then tossed each in the trash bin of his mind. He actually had no desire to die permanently, and less now than ever.

But here he was, closed up in a car with Terri's maddening scent and the all-too-recent memory of having drunk from her.

He shouldn't have done that. Resisting her had been hard enough all along, but now that he had tasted her, he was damn near lost. He didn't know why, but her blood had been like the finest champagne to him, finer than any he had ever drunk. Addicting. Nearly maddening him with desire for her.

His hands tightened on the steering wheel until he had to remind himself not to crush it. Because he could have.

Maybe he should beat his head on the steering wheel in hopes of pounding some sense into it. But no, he was quite sure that wouldn't work. Not anymore. Not with Terri's sweet blood singing in his veins. Making her part of him in a way he doubted he would ever be able to explain to her. When a vampire drank, it was no ordinary transfusion, no matter how Terri wanted to think of it.

It was one of the reasons he was so careful about who he drank from. He'd learned the hard way what it could cost to be indiscriminate. So he'd learned to take only from those who in some way were so empty that they affected him hardly at all.

But Terri wasn't empty. What's more, she was turning out to be a bit of a stubborn firebrand. Now that her blood ran in him, he was more aware than ever of her heartbeat, of her breaths, of her slightest reactions as they approached the dark streets of the warehouse district.

And more aware of the seriousness of the threat she posed to him.

Terri spoke. "Do all vampires hate themselves?"

The question took him aback. "What do you mean?"

"Well, I've heard how you talk about yourself. And then Creed said he didn't want his granddaughter to live your kind of life. So I wondered."

"No, we don't all hate ourselves. I'm not even sure hate is a good word. I think some of us despise what we could be. What we have been. But some of us, many of us, don't have any more qualms about following our natures than your kind do about eating meat."

He expected her to express horror or revulsion in some way, but she didn't. She sat there quietly thinking. He was beginning to understand that Terri thinking could be a problem in the making. For him, mostly.

So he waited, battling primal urges to finish what he'd started when he drank from her, urges to pull her into a dark alley and just have sex with her, and while he was at it to savor another half-pint of that champagne she called her blood.

Oh, he was definitely in danger of losing it. Of becoming what he most resisted and disliked.

"Is the way you've chosen to live so terribly hard for you?"

That was a question he'd have preferred not to answer, because he didn't want her to feel disgust for him. And yet, pushing her away might prove to be his saving grace. Whatever he wanted from her, most especially *because* he wanted it from her, the best thing would be for her to walk away. Now.

So he decided to answer as best he could, as truthfully as he could, even though his experience had no exact human parallel.

"I told you I'm a predator," he said.

"Yes."

"I meant it. That's what I am. Every instinct I have tells me to prey on you and other humans. And when I say you cannot possibly imagine how strong those urges are, I speak as one who was once human, once heir to all the weaknesses and desires of humankind. There is nothing, absolutely nothing, in your experience that even comes close to the urges I feel. I have a biological imperative, Terri, and it's to kill your kind."

She took that in silence. He waited for her to demand that he take her home, drop her on a street corner, get away from her. But the demands never came.

Finally she murmured, "But you fight it. That must be hard."

"Harder than you can imagine. Have you seen a tiger or a lion in the zoo?"

"Yes."

"Well, imagine that I'm that lion or tiger, locked in a cage of my own making, fighting my nature all the time."

"Oh, Jude." He thought her voice cracked. Then, "Letting you drink from me made it harder, didn't it?"

"More than you can know. I should never have done it."

"But why? Am I different from other people?"

"For me you are."

"In what way?"

He didn't want to answer this. He feared the truth. He didn't like to think why, but since Terri appeared in his life, that truth had been gnawing at the corners of his brain like a hungry rat.

"Not now," he said finally. "Not now."

He sensed her resistance to the put-off, but at last she settled back in her seat. He was about to pull away from the curb and continue the few remaining blocks to the warehouse district when his phone rang. He pulled it out and looked at it.

"Garner," he told her.

"Hey, man," Garner's voice said into his ear. "We're leaving the hospital now."

"Did you identify the scent?"

"Sort of. Jude?"

"Yeah?"

"This is a big one. Really big. Bigger than what we were hunting before."

"Great." He closed his eyes, wondering what level of the pantheon had found its way into this world again. "Anything else?"

"Yeah. You're not gonna like this, man."

"Just get to the point, Garner. I would absolutely love it if you would just get to the point."

"Sheesh, take it easy. Just don't blow up when I tell you."

"Tell me, for the love of heaven!"

"I smelled it before."

"When?" Jude closed his eyes, wondering how it was that Garner managed to be difficult no matter what he did or how he did it. The kid had an absolute genius for making *everything* more troublesome.

"Terri," Garner said. Jude could almost hear him wincing as he spoke.

"What about her, Garner? Will you just spit it out?"

"I, um, smelled it around her that night you saved her. So faint I didn't really pay attention."

"Well, that's hardly surprising if she confronted the same thugs."

"Right. Except...well..."

"Garner." Jude's voice held a note of threat.

"I smelled a whiff of it again tonight in your office."

Jude froze. He didn't speak a word, just sat staring into the night beyond the windshield. Finally, "On her? In her? Around her?"

"You want my opinion?"

"Damn it, I'm asking, aren't I?"

"It wasn't very strong. She's not infested. But if I smelled it again, then my guess would be something is following her."

Jude closed his eyes a moment. "Okay," he said. "We're almost to the warehouse district now. We'll wait for you there."

He snapped his phone closed, shoved it into his pocket, then gripped the steering wheel with both hands. His mind raced at a thousand miles an hour, trying to assemble pieces into some sort of idea or plan of action.

"Jude?" Terri's voice reached him. "What's going on."

His neck felt stiff as he turned to look at her. Not this woman, he thought. No matter what it took, they weren't going to get *this* woman, even briefly.

"Trouble," he said finally.

"What kind? Don't we already have enough trouble?"

He could tell she was trying to sound humorous. He didn't even bother to try to respond in kind. The question was how much to tell her and how to protect her.

And then he realized the most dangerous thing he could do was pull the punches. She had to know, she had to be aware. In a matter such as this, ignorance could be the most dangerous state of all.

"You remember I mentioned something about those thugs who accosted you smelling unnatural?"

She nodded. Even with as little light as there was, he could see her eyes widen.

"That same smell is on Creed's granddaughter."

"Garner smelled it?"

"Definitely. But there's more. Terri, I'm... sorry."

Her eyes grew even bigger, and he watched her draw one of those deep breaths that called almost primally to him, but as strong as his urges were, right now he found them easy to tamp because Terri was in danger.

Her voice sounded thin. "Just tell me, Jude. Please."

"Garner smelled it around you again to-night."

She sucked such a sharp breath it sounded deafening to him, although a human would find it quiet. "Is it… Am I…?"

He shook his head swiftly. "No. But that may be what's been following you."

"Oh. My. God."

She wrapped her arms around herself and squeezed her eyes shut. "It wants me?" The question was barely above a whisper.

"I don't know. Damn it, Terri, I don't know. But right now I'm thinking about taking you back to my place, away from the danger down here. I can't expose you."

"I'm already exposed!" Her eyes opened and they were filled with horror. "Jude, for the love of heaven, I told you I felt I was being watched. Followed. What does it matter *where* I am? You said I might be some kind of door-way. Or that I might have been marked some-how. But hiding me away is hardly going to deal with it, is it now?"

"The thing is," he argued back, "we don't know what we're dealing with here. Garner thinks it's more powerful than the demons I usually deal with. It's something we've never fought before."

"Then I guess we're going to have to learn how."

"No, you need to stay safely away."

"I think it's pretty obvious right now that I can't stay away!" Then her chin trembled and she whispered, "Oh, Jude…"

He might be a vampire, but that didn't mean he was impervious to a woman's distress. It didn't mean he was incapable of caring. Quite the contrary. He never bothered with seat belts, so he had only to release Terri's before he wrapped his arms around her, trying to surround her in a strength no human could imagine, a strength he had ever to be on guard not to use carelessly.

She curled into him in a way that tore at whatever heart a vampire had. Plenty of heart it seemed to him in those moments, as he felt the absolute rush of being turned *to* for protection, rather than away from.

God, the feeling could go to his head.

"Okay," he murmured. "Okay. We'll deal with this together. Garner can help at least some. And Creed. You're not alone, Terri. You're not alone."

Her fingers clutched at his leather coat. "Sorry," she whispered. "Sorry. It's just I'm remembering, and it's scary."

"That's all right. It *is* scary." To him perhaps most of all, because he knew what these things were capable of, and it was a helluva lot more than voices and a few scratches.

He felt a shudder ripple through her, and for once it didn't raise the predatory instincts he so loathed. No, it raised protective ones, stronger than he'd ever felt before.

He guessed he had something to thank a demon for. The thought was bitter, and made his mouth taste like bile, but he couldn't regret that overpowering urge to protect this woman.

He could have stayed there holding her indefinitely, but the night was waning in the way of nights, and he needed to meet Garner and Creed probably within a few minutes.

Reluctantly he eased his hold on Terri.

With what appeared to be equal reluctance, she pulled back and sat straight in her seat, staring into the darkness. "What should I do?" she asked, sounding surprisingly calm.

"I'd suggest some holy water." He stuffed his hand in his pocket and brought out the spray bottle. "May I?"

"Go ahead." She closed her eyes while he misted her everywhere he could. "Chloe's right," she said.

"About what?"

"You're going to have to train us all."

He didn't want to agree. He'd spent countless years keeping his assistants away from this kind of thing. Doing his level best to face the threat with other trained exorcists, like Father Dan. But now...

"I guess I am," he said harshly, then hit the accelerator harder than necessary, peeling them away from the curb with burning rubber, heading to the warehouse district.

He went straight for the place where Creed's granddaughter had been attacked. Not five minutes passed before Creed and Garner joined them. They climbed out of their vehicles and stood on the empty dark street while Garner walked around, his head lifted, sensing the night.

"It was here," he said finally. "But it's gone now."

"Any idea what direction?" Jude asked.

"We can drive around a bit, but I don't get a sense that it headed one way or another."

Jude frowned. "I've heard of such things."

Creed turned to him. "What have you heard?"

Jude shook his head. "This is hard to explain. Let's go back to my office."

Creed protested. "We haven't finished looking."

"For tonight we have. If Garner can't say which direction it went, then we need to do some research. We're dealing with the extraordinary here, Creed. Believe me. And I need to study and prepare."

Creed swore and turned, driving his fist into a brick wall. Terri gasped as brick crumbled. Creed didn't look as if the punch had even caused him a twinge.

No one said anything. Jude didn't even want

to try. He could imagine Creed's frustration and fury. Hell, he'd felt a form of it himself when Garner said he had smelled this *thing* around Terri.

Finally he gripped Creed's elbow. "Not tonight, Creed. I'll explain later, but I need to get Terri out of here."

"I agree, man," Garner commented. "This place has bad mojo for her."

Creed swore again then stomped back to his car. He paused just long enough to look back at Garner. "Come on," he said. "And stick your head out the window while we drive."

"Why? Do you smell that bad?"

"No, you do." Creed shook his head. "Just sense the air, Garner. Keep looking. That's what you do, isn't it?"

Garner muttered something but followed obediently.

"I think he's learning," Jude grumbled. Then he took Terri's elbow and guided her back to the car.

She surprised him by wrapping her arm tightly around his and leaning into him.

Too bad he couldn't enjoy it. Because it had

been centuries since a woman had last done that with him for any reason other than sex.

Back at the office, Jude glanced at the clock, even though he didn't really need to. The back of his neck had started prickling, however faintly. A glance at Creed suggested he wasn't the only one feeling the sun's approach.

"Will you explain *now?*" Creed demanded.

"As best I can." Jude had occupied Chloe's chair, Creed and Garner the couch, and Terri sat in the client chair at the end of Chloe's desk.

The thing was, he wasn't sure just how much he wanted to explain, or even should explain. Ideas had begun to knock around inside his head, ideas he was extremely reluctant to even entertain.

"Demons need a body to occupy in order to really act in this world. Without one, they're limited in what they can do. Hence possession. Having a body gives them the means to act here in ways they can't otherwise, and to do so with basic impunity because regardless of what happens to the body, it won't harm them. So by taking over a body, they can play their games much more broadly. Ugly games, usually, since they're nasty energies. Evil energies."

He looked around, making sure everyone had followed so far. Well, of course they had. There wasn't a stupid person in this group. Naive, maybe, but not stupid.

"Anyway," he went on, "for most demons, possessing a body is extremely difficult. So difficult that once they latch on to one, they're utterly reluctant to let go of it. That's the only reason possession is relatively rare. It isn't easy."

Terri spoke. "Why is it so hard?"

"Because, in order to take full possession, a demon has to find a willing, capable host. There doesn't necessarily have to be a conscious invitation, sometimes one is gained by trickery, or through a doorway of some kind that exists, but the demon must find access. And the host must offer something that the demon wants or needs, in terms of position, power, inclinations… Something that makes the host useful as more than a vehicle or there's simply no point in battling to take possession."

He knew these were difficult things to wrap the mind around—gateways, invitations, capabilities—but he received a chorus of nods. He was sure once they'd thought about it, they'd have questions. Hell, *he* still had questions.

"I don't claim to know everything," he continued. "The majority of demons I've encountered are fairly petty in their wants. They want the power of controlling a human body, they want to make mischief, they feed off pain. Their goals and desires seem to be immediate and short-term, which considering that they can burn out a human body pretty fast is probably the only reason most of them try to possess humans. Demonology 101, if you get me."

More nods. Okay. He hesitated, seeking words.

"These are the demons I'm familiar with. Once they occupy a body they're pretty much stuck there until they get cast out, the host dies, or the demon finds a way to take another body. Which, as I said, isn't easy. But I've heard there is another kind."

At that he certainly claimed their full attention. Even Creed leaned forward to listen intently.

"I've heard," Jude said carefully, "that there are demons with longer-range goals. These demons are supposedly more powerful, capable of transitory possession rather than the more permanent kind we see with lesser demons. Able to flit more easily between hosts. Like those thugs we're looking for. They'd be easy targets for a demon of that kind because they're obviously already twisted in some way which makes them amenable to temporary possession."

Garner leaned forward. "So you're saying this demon or demons could occupy those guys and then go as soon as the dirty work is done?"

Jude nodded. "I've heard of it, but never quite believed it. It's usually so hard for a demon to occupy a body that once they get one they don't let go willingly."

"But this is different," Terri said. She looked pale.

"That's how it looks to me. So I need to do some research. Get Chloe to work on it today. By tonight I should know at least something about how to attack this." He leaned back, feeling irritated by a bunch of things, not the least his concerns for Terri and Creed. "The hard part will be finding it. Garner, I don't care how tired you are, today I need you to go hunting."

"I will." Garner seemed to stiffen with resolve. "If it's anywhere out there, I'll find it."

"Do you still smell it around Terri?"

He shook his head. "No, it's gone."

One less thing to worry about. At least for now.

"Okay then," Jude said. "We meet tomorrow night at sunset, here."

Creed didn't move for a moment, but finally he stood. "I've got a little time. I'm going back to the hospital to look in on my granddaughter. Until tonight."

Then he glided across the room, almost too fast to see. At the door, he paused, looking back at Jude. "Do you see links?"

Jude nodded reluctantly. "Yes, Creed. And I don't like them."

"Neither do I." The only sign that he was gone was the closing door.

Jude noticed that Terri sat frozen. Garner, however, looked as if he was ready to leap in with questions. Jude was in no mood for them.

"Garner."

The young man's mouth snapped closed. Then he said, "Yeah?"

"Go home and get a couple of hours of sleep before you start hunting. And whatever you do, if you smell this thing don't get anywhere near it. Understand?"

Garner nodded. "I get it. And right now, I have no desire to get within range of it."

"But you'll look?"

"I'll look." Then he, too, rose and left.

Without looking at Terri, Jude picked up the phone and dialed. Chloe's sleepy voice answered him. "Hey, boss."

He guessed she had caller ID at home, too. "I need you in the office today. All day. I'll leave notes to get you started on some research."

At once she sounded more alert. "What's going on?"

"Something very, very bad. I'll do some research for as long as I can, but then I need you to take over."

"I'll be there."

When he hung up, he finally looked at Terri. She was staring at him. "What are you thinking?" he asked.

"I'm not sure. Except that there seem to be too many coincidences. Way too many."

His thoughts had been running along the same lines, but he refused to give voice to them. "Perhaps."

Maybe he was still a touch superstitious after all, as if speaking his thoughts aloud could make them happen. But right now, he had more important things to do than speculate.

"I'm going to research online," he said. "Why don't you try to nap on the couch? Or on the cot in the next room? You look beat."

After a few moments, she rose and went to lie on the couch.

But he noticed her eyes never closed.

Chapter 9

Terri couldn't close her eyes. *Demons capable of long-range planning.* What did that mean? How long a range? Years? Decades?

That feeling of being watched. Gone now. But there long enough to drive her back to Jude. Creed was connected to Jude, too, and his granddaughter had been attacked.

The coincidences left her cold as ice inside.

She listened to Jude typing away on the computer, with long pauses as he apparently read something, then the scribbling of a pen on paper as he made a note.

What she wanted, *really* wanted right now,

was to feel his arms around her again. Just as they had been in the car. Because they had made her feel safe, as if somehow Jude could be a bulwark against inchoate fears. Fears she didn't want to name. Fears that had haunted her childhood and now haunted her again.

What would a demon want with her? *Access.* But access to what?

And she must be out of her freaking mind. Only a couple of weeks ago she hadn't believed vampires existed. Now she had fed one and was looking to him for protection from *demons?*

She wouldn't even write that in a diary, if she had one, let alone say it out loud to anyone. Her world had turned so topsy-turvy, she didn't know which end was up anymore.

She had no idea how long she lay there, staring at the ceiling, trying to ignore uneasy, roiled thoughts.

How could vampires be real? She couldn't deny what she'd seen, what she knew, but she couldn't find a way to explain their existence. It flew in the face of everything scientific in her nature and training. How could he move so fast? How could he make people do things with a certain tone in his voice, or a certain look? How could he survive on blood alone? How could he be damn near immortal? All her training rebelled against what experience was teaching her. She wanted pigeonholes again, she supposed. Maybe when they got past this demon thing she could persuade him to talk to her, explain things at least as far as he understood them. That would probably help her a lot.

Right now, while her need for tidiness was useful in her job with the M.E., it helped her not at all with Jude.

All of a sudden, without a whisper of warning, Jude squatted beside her. She managed not to gasp her surprise, but she wondered if she'd ever get used to the way he could move so fast he almost seemed to materialize out of thin air.

"Time's getting short," he said quietly. "I left a list of things for Chloe to do when she comes in. Do you want me to take you home?"

Any drowsiness that might have been trying to sneak in vanished in an instant. "No!"

She thought he'd leave her there on the couch, but he surprised her. As if she weighed nothing at all, he slipped an arm beneath her shoulders, the other beneath her knees, and lifted her. The next thing she knew, they were on their way to his bedroom. So fast. He moved so fast the world passed in a blur.

Locks thunked behind them, then he gently set her on her feet in his bedroom. "Let me know now," he said. "You don't have to stay in here with me."

"Maybe I'll actually be able to sleep."

He withdrew his steadying arm and turned. She watched as he pulled open a drawer and took out a cleaner's shirt box.

"This'll cover you decently," he said as he handed it to her. "At least you'll be able to sleep comfortably."

She took the box and went into his bathroom. There, feeling sticky from a long day, she decided to use his shower and found the water cold. And it never warmed up. Sighing, she gave up and stepped under the cold pounding spray. When she'd finished washing, she stepped out and found a towel in a cupboard.

He was right about the shirt he gave her. Black silk like all his others, but with tails long enough to reach to her knees. She rolled up the cuffs to keep them out of the way, scooped up her clothes and stepped back into the bedroom. Jude lay on his bed, still fully clothed, having doffed only his boots and socks. Reaching over, he pulled the covers back so she could slide beneath them.

She did so hesitantly, aware that her heart accelerated. She saw his faint smile and knew that he heard it.

"This," he said, "might be the stupidest thing I've ever done." He pulled the covers up to her chin, then propped himself on an elbow, looking down at her.

"Stupid?" she repeated. If anyone here was being stupid, she figured it was herself. Here she was, preparing to sleep in the bed of a vampire who had admitted his basic instinct to prey on humans. One who had said he wanted her like hell on fire.

One she wanted equally as much.

"Soon," he said, "the sleep of death will take me. I can fight it off, but only for a while. So it won't be long before you'll be as safe as if I weren't in the room with you."

"Aren't I safe right now?"

"How safe do you want to be?"

Good question, she thought, as she stared back into his mesmerizing gaze. Her heart skipped and settled into a deep rhythm, the kind of rhythm her whole body wanted to feel. His golden gaze darkened.

"Jude," she whispered, then amazed herself by reaching up to cup his cool cheek. His skin felt so smooth, like satin, not like a mortal's skin. But nice. And she didn't mind the coolness at all because it wasn't icy. Later, while he slept, then he would feel like ice.

But now he was just cool, and smooth, and since she'd already had one brief experience of the world of desire he could transport her into, she felt a longing stronger than any she had ever known in her life.

His voice grew husky. "You don't know how dangerous this is."

"Then tell me."

But he didn't. Instead, he gave in to her longing, perhaps in to his own, and kissed her.

His cool tongue toyed with hers, teasing then encouraging the rhythm, echoing the beat of her heart until her entire body seemed to throb in time to the tempo.

"Have I told you how beautiful you are?" he whispered against her lips. "How desirable? Your scent alone was driving me mad before I ever set eyes on you."

His words caused another wave of longing to speed through her. Her eyes closed, and she clung to his strong shoulders, the only anchor left in her universe.

"Come to me, sweet one," he whispered. "Give yourself freely."

"I do," she managed to whisper back, not knowing what she was saying, just meaning whatever it was with every cell in her being.

She felt another coolness and vaguely realized the covers had been pulled down. Then a hand slipped up under the shirt she wore and cupped her yearning breast.

A soft cry escaped her at the contact and she arched, trying to press herself more firmly into his grasp. He kneaded her flesh with exquisite knowledge, knowing just how much and when.

Each squeeze, each brush of his thumb over her nipple, resounded throughout her entire body.

Then, finally, he took her nipple into his mouth and sucked. A ragged groan burst from her depths and her entire body bent toward him, wanting more.

Never had she felt so completely alive. She grasped the back of his head, holding him close, wanting him completely, more completely than she had ever wanted anyone.

His breath whispered against her heated skin, a delicious contrast. His lips and tongue toyed with her nipple as if he could feel exactly what she felt. Wordlessly she whimpered, greedy for even more. Greedy for complete possession.

"Easy, sweet one," he murmured before he brought his mouth to her other breast. Then delicious shock ripped through her as his hand slipped between her legs. At once she wanted to open herself to his touch, but at the same time she needed more and clamped her legs around his hand so that he could not pull it away.

He didn't even try. Knowing fingers stroked her, gently parting her petals, finding that exquisite knot of nerves.

She gasped as if there was no air left in the room. She arched into that touch helplessly, in thrall to need. Like a virtuoso, he played her, lifting her higher and higher, from the realm of the ordinary to a place so extraordinary she had never in her wildest imaginings conceived of it.

She ached. She throbbed. She pulsed. She wanted it to end, yet never end. Her hips rocked against his hand, rising and falling in a rhythm as old as time.

Yet he seemed to know just how to keep her at the pinnacle, drawing a deeper and deeper response from her until she nearly screamed her need.

Only then did he give her the touch that pushed her over into a shattering climax that left her blind and utterly without breath. Clenching ripples continued to run through her, as slowly, slowly, she drifted back to the mundane world.

When finally she could open her eyes a crack, she found Jude smiling at her.

"That was beautiful," he murmured.

"But...isn't there a missing part?" Her voice sounded thick, hoarse.

"You mean me?" He shook his head. "I got all I wanted from your experience. And I'm sorry, Terri, but it's time. Sleep now. We can talk later."

He lay back, his head falling on the pillow, and as she watched from heavy-lidded eyes, she saw him draw one deep breath and stiffen.

And then he was dead.

She reached out to touch him, wishing he could feel it. Wishing she could have given him even a portion of what he had just given her.

And then a funny thought struck her: *La petite mort*. Jude gave new meaning to the words.

Smiling, her entire body sated beyond words, she curled up under the covers, as close as she could get, watching him until at last sleep claimed her as well.

* * *

Life returned with a gasping breath, as it always did. In that instant, the pain he experienced was almost enough to make him scream. For him there was no wakening. Just life. Death to life in an instant, and it hurt. He had no sense that time had passed, no sense of waking. In one, single, microscopic instant, he returned, picking up his life exactly where he had left it the moment he had died again.

Only experience had taught him how to deal with the shock, how to accept that time had passed when he no longer had the mortal experience of sleep to tell him. No cell in his body remembered the hours when he had been dead. No dream teased at the edge of consciousness to remind him he had been here. His body even felt as if just this instant he had laid back on the bed.

And there was Terri, her blue eyes watching him, a faint frown between her brows. The idea that he might have left her frowning that morning, rather than feeling well-loved, caused him instant concern.

"What's wrong?" he asked.

"It hurts to come back, doesn't it?" she said quietly. "I saw it on your face when you took your first breath."

"Resurrection is always a shock. There's no warning. It's instantaneous, and every time it's shocking."

"Really? Do you dream?"

"No. Never."

Perplexity drew one corner of her mouth tight. "Do you miss it?"

"No. Not anymore."

She reached out and laid her hand on his chest. Feeling his heartbeat? His breaths? At least she wasn't shying from him, which meant he couldn't have screwed things up too royally that morning.

"Why—" She broke off sharply and suddenly looked embarrassed.

He rolled onto his side and drew her into his arms. "Ask me anything, sweet one. I'll answer if I can. Don't be shy."

"I was just wondering why…your saliva didn't numb me this morning when you kissed me."

"Ah." He drew her closer, for once allowing

himself to actually enjoy her luscious scent, dangerous or not. After all, it filled the room now and he couldn't escape it. But equally enticing was that he could still smell her orgasm, that heady odor that only came from lovemaking in humans. "That only happens when I expose my fangs. Otherwise, my saliva is fairly ordinary."

She tucked her head beneath his chin. "I guess that's a good thing."

"Well, it would sure muck up lovemaking if it were otherwise."

A muffled giggle escaped her, and at last he felt her relax. "Have you been lying here worrying about things?"

"Not really. I just have so many questions and I was feeling a little bad that I didn't give you what you gave me."

"But you did." Another moment to treasure, being able to stroke her hair and feel her face in his shoulder. Stolen moments that he'd pay for sooner or later, but he refused to worry about that now.

"How could I have?" she asked.

"Because I drank from you."

At that her head snapped up and she looked at him, astonishment framed on her face. "What do you mean?"

"I have an intense connection with you now. I can feel much of what you feel. I can't hear your thoughts, but you have no idea how much I can tell from your heartbeat, your scents, your sighs. And now that I've tasted you, I'm not only aware of those things, I feel them too when you're close."

She frowned. "But what about all the canned blood you drink? Does it connect you with everyone?"

"Not to this degree. Remember, it's been processed and tainted. It's some distance removed from the donor."

"But everyone you drink from fresh?"

"To some extent." But how to explain? "Terri, there are degrees of connection. If it's been a long time, then the connection fades. And I learned the hard way to choose my donors carefully. These days I usually try to find people who are not only willing to give to me, but who actually offer little in the way of a connection that would trouble me."

"But I'm different?"

"Very different. And that's the problem."

Unable to deal with continued inquisition in this particular area, he sat up and swung his feet to the floor. But even before he stood, she asked another question.

"Are you hurt because of me now?"

He closed his eyes and clenched his hands into fists. After a moment, he said, "I told you this was dangerous. Only time will answer your question."

Then he stood and headed for the bathroom, closing the door firmly behind him.

Amazing, he thought somewhere between frustration and amusement, but the bathroom had become his only sanctuary.

And he had no one to blame for that but himself.

Chloe eyed them with one lifted brow as they emerged into the outer office together. "Well, well."

"Don't, Chloe," Jude said. "I could get snappish."

"Nothing new in that, Boss."

"Do you want to embarrass Terri?"

Terri felt her cheeks stain red. She was already a bit embarrassed.

"Oh, *certainly* not!" Chloe answered. "Never that. But she looks like something the cat dragged home. Clothes? A hot shower? Men!"

Terri felt Jude look at her. "It's okay," she said quickly. "I managed a cold shower. As for clothes…"

"Somebody," Chloe said, "ought to take you home to change. *Somebody* ought to think about installing a water heater."

"Somebody," Jude answered, "has indeed been remiss."

Chloe rolled her eyes at him. "Do you want the news or not?"

"Sure. And make sure to get a plumber out here soon to put in a water heater."

Chloe looked at Terri. "Four years," she said. "For four years I've been taking icy showers when I've had to stay here for days on end because of a case."

"You should have said something," Jude retorted. "Damn it, Chloe, I don't read minds and I haven't really noticed temperature in nearly two hundred years."

Chloe now arched both brows. "Really?"

"Really."

She hitched one shoulder in a sort of shrug. "Well, I can understand why you wouldn't think of it then."

Jude's tone grew sarcastic. "So I'm forgiven?"

"I'll think about it. Now, on to the news. Creed called just a few minutes ago. He's going to be late. Something about his granddaughter in a crisis."

"Hell," Jude said quietly. "How bad?"

"He didn't say. And since when do vampires have grandchildren?"

"Since they married and sired children *before* they became vampires!"

Chloe pulled her head back a bit at Jude's frustrated tone. "Sheesh. Okay. Cool your freaking jets, or whatever antiquated slang you understand. The rest of the news?"

"Please," he said between his teeth.

"Garner didn't find anything. He said he'll

look until he gets too tired and then start again in the morning."

Terri watched the exchange, wondering what had put Chloe so much on edge. Jealousy? Hadn't she said she had long since gotten over her fascination with Jude? But what if she hadn't? Terri squirmed uncomfortably.

Chloe, however, presented the answer a moment later. "I did the research you wanted. At least as much as I could." She pointed across the room to a stack of very old books. "I even hit some rare-book stores. You read fast, right?"

"Right."

"Good. Because just from the little I've managed to pull together today in addition to what you learned last night, I'd say we're in serious trouble, boss."

"I thought that was likely."

"No, are you hearing me, Jude? *We,* as in *all* of us, are in serious trouble!" Chloe rose from her chair. "You'd better start training us all. Fast. Because from what I've learned so far, one of us—Garner, me, you, Creed, or Terri—is the target."

Terri sank onto the couch, suddenly light-headed and weak. Chloe hurried across the room to sit beside her. "Jude, what did you do? *Drain* her?"

"No!" The answer came simultaneously from both Jude and Terri.

"She looks awful. Maybe sleeping in your coffin with you isn't restful for a human."

Terri shook her head. "I'm *fine,* Chloe. Just...frightened."

"Ah, a wise person in the bunch." Chloe patted her hand. "Someone who sees the dangers here. You're a marvel, Dr. Black. You've probably noticed by now that Jude believes he's invincible. I suspect Creed labors under the same delusion. Garner is every bit as cracked, too. You and I need to restore some sense here."

In spite of the chill creeping along her spine, Terri had to smile. "There's plenty of sense to go around, Chloe. Jude was the first to recognize the seriousness of the threat."

Chloe sighed. "And here I was enjoying thinking I was on top of things first for a change."

A snort escaped Jude.

Chloe ignored him. "We've got to get you some fresh clothes."

"I don't want to go back to my apartment. At least not alone. That thing may be following me."

Chloe's eyes widened. "What makes you think that?"

"I've been feeling watched for a while now. And Garner said he could smell it around me, very faintly. As if it had come and gone."

Chloe looked at Jude. "Not good."

"Do you think I don't know that? It's the main reason she stayed here last night. I wasn't about to let her go home."

"No ulterior motive, huh?"

Terri shook her head. "Chloe, please. Jude offered me my choice of where I wanted to sleep. I didn't feel safe alone in the outer office."

"Well." Chloe frowned. "I guess I can understand that. After what I read today, I don't want to be alone, either. I thought Jude would *never* come out of there."

Jude pulled a chair over, sitting closer to the two women. "I agree neither of you should be alone. So here's what we'll do. We'll get you both some clothes, enough for a few days. Then I'll get you a meal and bring some food back here."

Chloe groaned. "Oh, joy, a campout."

"Would you prefer to go home?"

"No."

Which seemed to settle the issue.

Jude went to get his coat, and Terri watched as he checked all his pockets to ensure he had the tools of his trade. Then he pulled out a spray bottle of holy water.

"Hey, I'm sort of a Wiccan," Chloe protested, but she nevertheless submitted to the spraying, muttering to Terri, "White magic is white magic."

Outside in the evening darkness, with the air feeling as soft as satin, they piled into Jude's car with Chloe in the backseat.

"I'd better warn you both," Jude said, "but I can't handle brightly lighted stores for long. So if you want me to stay with you, this is going to have to be as fast as you can make it."

"Fluorescent lighting bothers you?" Terri asked.

"If it's bright. My eyes are extremely sensitive. And if a place uses full-spectrum lighting, it's painful to my skin."

"We'll be fast," she promised. "I'm not shopping for fancy. If it would be easier on you, we could just run by my place and I could get my own stuff."

He reacted instantly. "No, I don't think that would be wise."

Chloe leaned forward until her head was almost between them. "Go to the mall on Brownville Avenue. There's a clothing store there with an outside entrance. We can be in and out fast, and the place isn't as bright as a mega store."

"Good idea," Terri said. "I still don't know my way around town enough to even know of a place like that."

"How long have you been here?" Chloe asked.

"About six weeks. I came from Chicago."

"A big-city girl."

"Only recently. Before that I lived in a really small town. This place is as big a city as I ever want to live in."

"It's big enough," Chloe agreed. "I find everything I want here."

"And a few things you don't," Jude remarked.

Terri cocked her eye his way. "You *had* to bring that up."

They shopped rapidly. All either of them wanted were some comfortable slacks, a few lightweight shirts, a jacket and underwear. Lots of clean underwear. The clerk allowed Terri to change into one of her new outfits in the dressing room, which made her feel considerably better.

Jude paid at the register for all of it, then carried their bags to the car where he put them in the trunk.

"Now," he said, "a quiet, dark restaurant, preferably one where we won't have to spend most of the evening. What kind of food would you like?"

Chloe looked at Terri. "Chinese or Italian?"

"Italian. Less animal fats."

Chloe sighed. "I knew there had to be a downside to knowing a doctor."

"There's a downside to having a vampire

as your host, too," Jude remarked. "I haven't scoped out any restaurants."

So Chloe guided them to a small restaurant with dim lighting that wasn't terribly busy. "The food's passable," she said. "But you want fast service so we're stuck with a place that isn't real popular."

"Maybe we should just get takeout," Terri suggested.

Both Chloe and Jude instantly looked at her, alarm clearly evident on Terri's face.

"Something wrong?" Jude asked.

"Not really. I never used to be agoraphobic, but right now I'm feeling exposed. Silly, I guess."

"Not silly." His eyes were darkening again. "Maybe takeout would be the best thing."

"It would save you having to pretend to eat," Chloe retorted, but she quickly wrapped her arm around Terri's shoulders. "Takeout it is. I'm in no mood to ignore anyone's feeling of uneasiness."

"Neither am I," Jude replied.

Forty-five minutes later, back at the office,

Chloe and Terri ate at the desk while Jude went into his office to make some calls.

"I don't like this at all," Chloe told Terri. "I mean, I've always known what Jude deals with, but it's never seemed threatening to me before. So he exorcises people. Hard for him, no problem for me. I'm safely away from the action. But not this time." She shook her head.

"What did you learn today that got you so worked up?"

"There's this kind of demon I've never heard of before. Some call it a hunter demon. It's after one specific thing."

"Which is?"

Chloe shrugged. "It varies. But it's a weird kind of demon because it can manipulate lots of people to get what it wants. It's not just looking for any old thing it can get. It wants *one* thing. And there've been cases where groups of people have been brought together in order to set the stage for the demon getting what it wants."

Terri lost interest in eating. She put her fork down. "How do we know what it wants?"

"We don't. Not yet. But after reading that

stuff, I started to get creeped out. Too many coincidences."

"That's what I said last night."

"You, too?" Chloe looked down, pushing penne around on the bottom of her foam container. "Too bad we don't know what it wants. Or how it thinks."

"Is that what had you so edgy when we got up?"

"Yeah." She looked up from her dinner and met Terri's gaze. "I wasn't jealous or anything, if that's what you're thinking. A few years ago, I might have been, but I got over it. Jude's too old for me."

That surprised a short laugh from Terri. "What?"

"Seriously. I work hard at not growing up too much. He's lived more than two hundred years, and I know I strike him as a kid. Garner, too. Most especially Garner. Jude treats him like a troublesome son. And sometimes I think he feels the same about me. Although of course I'm not nearly as much trouble as Garner."

Terri smiled. "No, you're definitely not."

A grin answered her. "Anyway, I can see you don't strike him that way. So if you and he get something going, you won't hear any whining from me. He's got friends, both vampire and human, but sometimes I wonder if he's lonely, anyway." She shrugged one shoulder. "Of course, what do I know? Maybe vampires don't get lonely. Most of them seem to prefer solitude from what I've seen."

"And most of us," Jude said from the doorway of his office, "could have heard that conversation from halfway across town."

Chloe made a face at him. "Eavesdropper."

"With my hearing, it's hard not to. Creed says his granddaughter seems to be pulling through the crisis, so we may well see him in a few hours. Garner has promised to be here before dawn to keep an eye on you, Chloe."

"Oh, great. Protection from Garner. I may as well hang myself now."

"It's better than nothing. You know I can't stay awake to do it myself. I would if I could. But I'll teach you both a few things tonight for self-protection, and you know that Garner would smell the thing coming."

"What good will that do if you're asleep?" Chloe asked.

"Chloe, you know I can't stay awake. At most I can only wake in short bursts."

"I know." Chloe sighed. "I'd just like something better than Garner to depend on."

"I'll see that you have it. Before this night is over, I'm going to seal this office in every way I know."

Chapter 10

Chloe complained that she was getting sleepy, having arrived at work shortly after dawn.

"Go get some sleep then," Jude said. "On the cot, on the couch. You'd probably sleep better tonight than tomorrow."

"Oh, definitely. Tomorrow you'll be dead and I'll be relying on Garner." Chloe cleaned up the leftovers, putting them in a refrigerator in the kitchenette, then made her way to the small room that contained a cot. "When the demon breaks the door down, be sure to wake me. I wouldn't want to miss anything."

Terri turned to Jude, wishing she could just

walk into his arms and feel his embrace again. Then she pushed the longing away. One act did not a relationship make, she reminded herself. And anyway, how sure was she that she wanted to get any more emotionally involved with a vampire?

Chloe was right, and if Chloe didn't claim to understand a vampire's emotional needs, how could she truly be involved after just a few short weeks that added up to actually very little time with him?

Get a grip, girl, she told herself. Almost the instant she had the thought, Jude seemed to frown at her. Then his face smoothed over and he went to pick up the stack of books Chloe had purchased earlier.

"I'll be in my office reading," he said.

Leaving her to sit there like a fifth wheel. Not a thing to do except ponder a million questions, and the strange world she had entered when Jude had rescued her from those creeps.

Being alone with her own thoughts didn't seem to be the wisest choice right now.

Then she remembered what he had said about being so closely connected with her since drinking from her. Had he felt her withdrawal as a rejection?

The thought brought her instantly to her feet. She might have questions about a lot of things, including what a vampire really was, and whether she wanted to get any more involved with one, but she also knew one thing for certain: she didn't want to hurt him.

She hurried to the door of his office and saw him reading. Pages in the book flipped so fast a breeze might have been blowing them. Astonishment drove other thoughts from her mind for a second. Then she asked, "Are you really reading that fast?"

He glanced up. "Yes."

The pages resumed flipping.

Oh, she had hurt him. "Jude, before…" But what could she say?

He looked up again, his face revealing nothing.

Finally she blurted, "I wasn't rejecting you!"

"I don't know what you mean." Cool, composed.

"I think you do." She walked into his office

and closed the door behind her. "I'm still trying to adjust, that's all. You're different."

"Tell me something I don't know."

"What I mean is, I don't know what it means to be a vampire. What it means to be you. What you feel. What you need. Heck, I'm still having trouble at times *believing* what you are, and I've certainly seen enough that you would think that wouldn't be a problem anymore."

The pages stopped flipping. After a moment, he put the book aside, open, and sat back. He folded his hands and gave her his full attention.

The full attention of a vampire, particularly a vampire named Jude, was enough to make her heart skitter and race, and her mouth grow dry.

"Take a seat, Terri," he said quietly.

Her legs felt jerky as she walked over and took the chair facing his desk. She knew this was going to be awkward and possibly frightening. But right now understanding Jude seemed far more important to her than understanding a demon. Maybe the feeling was foolish, but it ruled her right now.

"Ask," he said. "I've told you before. Just ask."

"I know so little. I don't understand how you can exist."

"Neither do I, but I do. And many others like me. We exist just as you do. Our births, if you can call them that, are the main difference. That and the fact we die every damn day, like it or not. But I can't answer your scientific questions. They're impossible."

"I know. It bugs me because of my background, not to understand how you can be."

He nodded, tightening his lips.

"But," she said finally, "I'm learning to live with that. Would I love to analyze a sample of your blood and DNA? Of course. But if I did that, I couldn't do it secretly, and that might put you in danger."

"Thank you for recognizing that."

"I don't want to endanger you, Jude."

Again he nodded.

"But I need to know you. I need to know

about you. How different are you from me? Do you even have the same feelings?"

His gaze darkened, and when he spoke his voice was quiet, controlled. "I have the same feelings as you, Terri. Every one of them. I even have some extra ones I've mentioned. But the ones I have that are like yours?"

"Yes?"

"They're a hundred times stronger."

"Oh." Her heart fluttered nervously. "That could be...bad." She said it uncertainly. The things she felt for Jude were already strong enough to scare her, especially when they were for a creature who wasn't human. At least not in the way she thought of human.

"I scare you," he said flatly.

"Not you," she said quickly. "The idea that you feel things so strongly."

"I don't always feel things that strongly. Most things in life we don't feel much at all. Think of your average day, Terri. How much emotional energy do you expend on most things?"

"Little enough," she admitted.

"So multiplied by a hundred isn't so very much, is it?"

"Maybe not. But isn't it hard to feel so strongly?"

"It's a saving grace, actually."

That piqued her curiosity and she leaned forward. "How so?"

"Do you think centuries of existence could even be tolerated if the days slipped by without the spice of emotion? And my life is well-spiced. Spiced beyond your imaginings."

"Can you explain? Give me an example?"

One corner of his mouth lifted. "It's hard because you've never experienced it. But let me try. Imagine living life with a veil over everything, dulling colors, dulling sounds, dulling feelings. As if you were mildly drugged."

"Okay."

"Then imagine having that veil ripped away. That's what it's like for me. A veil was ripped away when I changed. Everything is sharper, sweeter, more colorful. A symphony of textures. In fact, a symphony I enjoyed as a human is a hundred times more beautiful to me now, every note of the orchestra as clear as the purest bell." He paused, then added wryly, "As long as the orchestra is good."

"So it's not painful?"

"It can be, but the good more than makes up for the bad. When I go out at night and look up at the heavens, I see more than pinpricks of light in the sky. I see their full spectra. I see colors you can't. When I see a rainbow, I see shades and hues you never will. I see more stars than you can. I not only see people as you do, but I see the energy they emanate."

"Auras?"

"Perhaps. I don't know if that's what psychics see. I only know what I see, and it's beautiful. I can hear the harmonics in your voice rather than the muddle I would have heard as a human. You have one of the loveliest voices I've heard in my two centuries. When I watch you walk, I feel an incredible appreciation for your grace. Things I never would have noticed before I notice now. Like the intoxicating scent that surrounds you. No human would even notice it."

She nodded, beginning to grasp it, at least a little. "But you're talking about your senses."

"And you want to talk about my emotions."

"Yes." An almost timid agreement.

He fell into thought, as if trying to find a point of comparison. Eventually, he spoke, his voice as deep and dark as rich velvet. "When I was still human, I tossed my heart around freely. I must have fallen in and out of love with the phases of the moon. I dallied freely with the ladies, and moved on quickly. It embarrasses me now, but perhaps I can blame it on youth and war."

"War?"

"I spent half of my human life at war, in the army. When you're often unsure you'll still be alive the end of the next day, you value things differently."

"I guess I can understand that. Sometimes after working a truly ugly case I get that feeling."

He smiled faintly. "It has a tendency to heighten your pleasure-seeking."

"Or your need to find a way to forget."

"True. Regardless, I was rather careless about others. When my own heart got broken, it tended to heal relatively easily. As for the warring itself, well, it made me feel intensely alive. Which is not to say it wasn't ugly, but you know what adrenaline can do, especially when added to the sense that your time may be very short."

"I can imagine."

"When I turned, I became driven by emotions I couldn't control because they overwhelmed me. They ruled me. I had thought I knew anger, love and lust, greed, hatred and hunger. I had no idea."

Terri tried to envision it, but was certain she got only the barest glimmer.

"I had appetites I couldn't control, needs I couldn't understand. And I'll be honest, Terri. Years passed before I ceased to be a slave to my emotions and appetites. Self-control isn't an emotion, it's a choice. And even now, after practicing it for more years than I really care to count, it's not perfect."

"And now?"

"Now what?"

She didn't know how to ask. Indeed, she was afraid of what he might say.

He was the one who spoke first. "I keep telling you this is dangerous."

"Then maybe you should tell me why."

He sighed heavily and leaned back. "I guess I should. Because I still want you like hell on fire, that's not going away in the least little bit, so you'd better know what it might mean."

"And that is?"

"A claiming."

She waited, but he seemed reluctant to say more, so finally she pressed him. "What does that mean?"

"Vampires are extremely territorial. As a rule you won't find us in very close proximity to one another. Yes, we can be friends, just as Creed and I are, but as a rule, we're solitary because territoriality can make us dangerous to each other."

"Okay. I get that. It even makes survival sense. You wouldn't want to be too close together because it could reveal your existence."

"Maybe. Whatever it is, it *is*. Yes, we have friends, yes, we even occasionally have parties, although I've grown tired of most of them. Imagine a nightclub run amok until the wee hours."

"I don't think I'd like that much."

"I know I don't. But even vampires have a need to socialize sometimes. So we find others of our kind the same way you humans do, people we find agreeable. We form networks, and sometimes even groups we call families. I would consider Creed, for example, to be family."

"I'm glad. Glad to know you're not completely alone."

"Oh, I'm not alone. You've noticed Chloe and Garner, and there are others, as well, human and vampire both. Not a large group, but enough for my needs."

She noticed he seemed to be trying to avoid explaining what a claiming was, and she wondered if she should press him or let it slide. Everything in its own time, she cautioned herself.

But Jude apparently decided to just plunge in. "Claiming," he repeated. "It's a very different thing from socializing. It doesn't happen often, but when it does, it can be deadly."

"Deadly?" The word took her aback, it was so unexpected.

"Deadly," he repeated emphatically.

Her mouth felt dry again, something about the way his dark eyes stared at her.

"We call it a claiming. No one knows how it happens or why. But then we don't know the how or why of much of our existence, so what's one little thing more? Only this is no little thing."

She licked her lips. "What is it?"

"When we claim something or someone, a bond is forged, an unbreakable one. That thing or person becomes *ours*. We will not let it go. If two vampires claim the same thing it usually leads to one of them killing the other."

"Oh, my!"

"Well, it gets worse. Most claiming occurs between vampires. That's okay unless only one of them makes the claim."

"But if only one does?"

He closed his eyes a minute. "Terri, let me put this in frank, simple terms, so you know the danger you're running here. If I claim you, I will not be able to let you go. You can fly to the farthest part of the planet and I'll follow you. If you don't want me, I will become your worst nightmare. You won't be able to shake me."

"You'd stalk me?" The thought horrified her.

"Actually," he said heavily, "I think that before I ever did that to you, I'd kill myself."

He expected her to jump up, to say she was leaving. He'd seen the play of emotions on her face, had smelled her changing scents as she reacted. He'd known the moment when she felt horror.

But she couldn't run, not with the threat that seemed to be stalking her. How in the hell could he protect her from that thing and from *himself?*

She said, her voice cracking, "You think... you think you might claim me?"

"It's been a concern at the front of my mind since I met you. No one has ever affected me the way you do, Terri. No one. Don't ask me to explain it. These things have no explanation.

But now you know exactly the kind of fire we're playing with here."

"That's why you wanted me to go away at first."

"Exactly."

"Then for your sake I should go."

For *his* sake? "Terri, you can't. There's a demon out there following you."

"So? Do you really think I care so little about you that I'd play with your life?"

But she would play with *hers?* "No," he said, putting as much force into the word as he could. "You're not going anywhere. I won't have you on my conscience."

"But if this claiming thing happens—"

He cut her off. "Then I'll deal with it."

"Not by killing yourself. Do you think I want that on my conscience?"

Serious as the discussion was, errant humor trickled through him. "Most of your kind would agree that fewer of my kind would be a good thing."

"Cut it out, Jude. You know *I* don't think that."

"Not anymore, but I still shock you and disturb you. And even horrify you."

He watched the struggle play across her face, smelled her inner uneasiness and worry. But amazingly, he felt no loathing from her.

She chewed her lip for a moment and he wished he could do that for her. Gentle nibbles. Nibbles that would transport her until she gave herself to him as she had just before sunrise this morning. Those moments of magic lingered with him even more than they did with her. Indelible moments, ones he would never be able to forget, and all the more priceless because she hadn't chosen to do it because he was a vampire. Hadn't given herself because he had vamped her with fascination.

He wished he could toss away all his other concerns and carry her to his bed again, this time to take away the layers of concealment he'd left between them last night, to strip her to her skin and drink in her every inch with his eyes, his hands, his mouth. To let her discover him the same way, partly because it had been a long time since he'd allowed a woman to do that, and partly because he wanted Terri to know him that way. Just Terri.

And therein lay the rub, he thought bitterly. He wanted more than he'd wanted from a woman ever before. Maybe that's what made him so dangerous.

"Promise that you won't kill yourself," she said finally.

It was easy enough to promise, because he'd make sure she would never know if it came to that. "You aren't disturbed by the thought that I might haunt you for the rest of your days?"

"Less disturbed than I would be if you killed yourself. I know you wouldn't hurt me."

"Well, then, I promise."

He watched her relax, apparently satisfied that the situation would somehow be manageable. If it happened. Little did she know.

Then he saw another question dawn on her face. A split second later it was followed by hesitation.

"Terri?"

"Yes?"

"I drank from you. I made love to you. I

think we've reached a point where you can ask any question you want."

She flushed a bit, and of course had no idea how that called to him. His hunger awoke, and he thought about getting a bag of blood to silence it. But no, nothing would silence the siren call of fresh blood pumping through warm veins, especially when the blood in question had been the most exquisite he had ever tasted. He could wait. He had schooled himself to wait.

"This claiming," she said. "Is it like love? Only magnified?"

He smiled faintly. "I don't know. I've never experienced it. I suspect that would be the closest human parallel, though. The main difference I can see is that it never fades. It never pales. Chloe calls it 'new relationship energy,' that rush humans get in the first throes of love."

"I've felt it."

"Every thought, every breath seems to revolve around the person you love. The world becomes bright and fresh, feelings are intensified, you ache until you meet again, you can think of little else."

"Been there. Once. Briefly."

"Well, from what I can tell, a claiming is much the same except that it never weakens. Never becomes a quieter feeling."

"Like a compulsion?"

"Perhaps."

And he realized he had really had enough. He had sat here calmly discussing these matters as if they were no more than the weather, when indeed they were a tsunami, a hurricane, a major earthquake. The vampire version of a huge natural disaster.

All the while he'd been doing it, he'd been fighting his instincts, fighting his hunger, fighting his lust. Feelings on a scale that beggared any human experience.

His control slipped. Before she could blink he was on the other side of the desk, reaching for her. He half-expected her to pull back in shock, because she couldn't possibly have seen him move, but she didn't. When his hands touched her shoulders, she rose toward him, not away. She let him wind her in his arms, and when he buried his face against her neck, he felt her cradle the back of his head.

Unbelievable.

It would have been so easy to take her then. With one little lick, he could numb her throat, and then with one small bite he would feel her heartbeat inside himself as she nourished him with her very life. He could once again taste that champagne.

He leaned back against his desk, drawing her into the cradle between his thighs, letting her know that in one way he was just like any mortal man. She gave a small gasp and let her head fall back even more as she pressed herself against him, giving him an answer in the timeless language of the body.

For an instant, his brain seemed to turn into a red haze of need, just one instant, one thought away from frenzy.

Then he caught himself, nuzzling her, drawing in her scent until it filled his lungs.

"Why don't you?" she whispered.

"Because," he whispered back, "longing is such a sweet ache."

"Maybe when you have centuries. Not so much when you only have decades."

He laughed almost soundlessly, then drew another lungful of her heady scent before lifting his head. Searching her blue eyes, seeing they looked sleepy with the same passion he was feeling, he couldn't help but smile.

"Unfortunately," he said, brushing a strand of her dark hair back behind the delicate shell of her ear, "we have important things to be concerned about tonight."

She sighed. Her sweet breath reached him, heightening his longing. It was hard, so hard to cling to his self-control.

"This is important, too," she said, but she sounded regretful as if she knew he was right. She tipped her face up and brushed a kiss against his lips. Then he loosened his hold on her as she stepped back.

"I did promise Chloe protection," he said.

"You did," she agreed.

"Much easier to provide when my office door is open."

"It certainly is."

Then before he could forget himself, he

whisked across the room to open the door. He looked back to see Terri frowning.

"What?" he asked.

"I'm just wondering if I'll ever get used to the way you can move. It's disorienting." Then her frown vanished and she smiled.

God, what a smile. He'd follow that to the ends of the earth, too, if he wasn't careful. Right to perdition.

Creed arrived about two in the morning. Garner appeared to be sleeping off a long day at his place, but he had promised to show by dawn.

"How's your granddaughter?" Jude asked Creed.

"Better. Much better. The crisis passed and the improvement is remarkable."

"I'm glad." Simple words that conveyed a wealth of feeling.

"So what have you learned?" Creed asked. He settled on the couch again. Jude was already at Chloe's desk, and Terri had decided to sit on an armchair farther away. She wasn't sure why, but just now she felt a reluctance to be close to Jude. Maybe that claiming idea had disturbed her more than she realized. Imagine being hunted by a vampire for the rest of your life, if you decided you didn't want to be his?

At the same time, she wanted Jude beyond anything right now, and had the feeling that given just a tiny bit more time, she might become as obsessive about him as he was afraid of becoming about her.

Just looking at him made her ache with deep yearning, and some dastardly voice in her mind kept asking: But do you really want to love a *vampire?* Maybe not, but love was seldom a choice. Of course she wasn't in love yet. She couldn't be.

"What I've learned," Jude said, "is that one of these things is no real threat to you or me."

"Really." Creed arched a brow. "How is it we're so fortunate?"

"I don't know. However it is, for this kind of demon to possess either you or me would be as hard, if not harder, than an ordinary demon taking over a human."

"Ordinary?" Terri spoke, feeling a slither of astonishment. "How can any demon be ordinary?"

Jude cocked a brow at her. "It's a relative thing."

"I guess it must be."

"So," Creed asked, "what is it after?"

"Either you or me."

Shocked, Terri felt as if the room turned suddenly cold. "How can that be? Garner said it was following *me*. I felt it."

"Have you felt it following you since you walked in on me doing that exorcism?"

"No."

Jude spread his hands. "My guess is that you felt compelled to follow me that night because of that demon. It was hoping you'd be weak, that you'd open a door, distract me, make me vulnerable in some way. But it didn't happen. Because you're strong."

"So it couldn't use me to get at you?"

"Apparently. Now it's trying another angle with Creed." He looked at his friend. "My guess is that it wants a vampire, any vampire. If you had gone after it by yourself, it might have found a way to anger you into inviting it in. Instead, you came here. You exercised restraint. So it hasn't gotten at you, either."

"But why a vampire?" Terri asked.

"Oh, to possess an immortal body," Creed said bitterly. "So my granddaughter nearly died so that it could get at me in a weakened state. I'd like to send that thing back to the pits of hell."

"It may be attracted to our immortality," Jude agreed, "but it may be more. I don't have to tell you what kind of instruments of terror and death we can become."

Creed's face darkened, but he nodded. "There are those out there in the night who already do such things. Why not one of them?"

"Perhaps," Jude said, "because they don't care. No wedge."

Creed swore.

Terri felt as if a knife were driving into her heart. She had to draw a deep breath to steady herself. "So it's looking for targets that you two care about."

"For all I know," Jude said, "it may have attacked you that night simply because it knew I was in the area and would respond. And maybe it sensed how attracted I was to your scent. I certainly noticed it *before* you were attacked by those thugs."

Terri nodded but said nothing. She'd rolled with a lot of shocks to her worldview in a relatively short time span, and just as she was getting her feet under her, coming to accept vampires, one in particular, and the idea that a demon may have been the source of her terrified childhood, one that may have come back to haunt her again, now things were turning topsy-turvy again.

"So you're saying that a demon may have caused those guys to threaten me in order to get your attention."

"Something like that. I mean, your scent already had my attention, but I would have moved on had I not heard you cry out and then smelled your fear."

"Fear," Creed remarked, "is an almost irresistible call."

"It is?" Terri felt her jaw drop. *"Fear?"*

"Yes." Jude bit the word off.

Terri watched him in pained puzzlement, trying to understand. Why would these beings be drawn to fear? That disturbed her at some deep level, and she couldn't help her response. But she could also see that in some way Jude had pulled back from her, as if he felt she had judged him.

Had she? Maybe. God, it was as if she were peeling back a veil all of a sudden. As if she had forgotten what he was over the last few days, and now she was seeing him in contrast to what she considered human. And humane.

But, another part of her argued, even humans could be incredibly inhuman. Hadn't she seen enough evidence of that in her work? Jude had done nothing, nothing at all, to prove himself inhumane. In fact, he had told her he struggled with urges beyond the ordinary in order *not* to become a monster.

The conversation had swirled on around her, and she didn't become aware of it again until Creed announced he needed to go back to the hospital and would see them that evening.

Alone with Jude, Terri found him looking at her intently. Her skin prickled with awareness. Had anyone ever looked at her that way, with so much hunger, so much wariness?

What could he have to fear from her? Plenty,

she thought glumly. He'd probably smelled her every reaction, her every doubt, felt her response to everything he'd said. Hadn't he told her that since drinking her blood he was intimately aware of her in ways she was certain she couldn't begin to imagine?

"Jude…"

He shook his head. "No, Terri. No need to explain or apologize. I know what I am, and it's only natural that you should question yourself and me. I'd be more concerned if you didn't."

"Why?"

"Because I couldn't trust you. I'd have to believe you don't know what you're doing. So it revolts you that I respond to fear?"

Feeling small somehow, she just looked at him.

"Well, it revolts me, too. But it's my nature. If I let myself, I can get high from instilling fear. How else do you think I could be a predator?"

"I don't know."

"Tell me something honestly."

"If I know the answer."

He leaned a little toward her. "Hasn't your arousal been heightened occasionally by fear?"

She gasped, instinctively wanting to deny it. But she couldn't. The first time he had inhaled her scent while standing behind her sprang immediately to her mind. And there were other times. Moments when fear and arousal had trickled through her simultaneously. "Yes."

He leaned back. "I thought so." But he didn't sound satisfied, just accepting. "It's just a matter of degree."

As a doctor, she could define the connection, too. She looked down at her hands then back at him. "I understand. But for you someone else's fear is the key?"

"It can be."

"So that's different."

"Fear calls to me. That doesn't mean I have to act on it. But my response is what it is."

He stood up so quickly she barely saw him move. The next thing she knew he was standing in the doorway of his office. "Garner will be here in an hour or two to watch Chloe. I'll leave my door open. Just be sure to lock me in at dawn."

Chapter 11

He lay on his bed, still dressed, wondering how Terri was going to take this. He was a fool to have ever let her get this close. In fact, he should have listened to himself to begin with when he thought he needed his head examined.

He knew what he'd just revealed to her and understood her response to it. It revolted him, too. It was one of the impulses he hated most in himself. But he couldn't deny it existed. And if Terri was going to remain in his life, for however long or short a period, she needed to know exactly what she was dealing with: a vampire, not simply a human who didn't age.

Sometimes, though not as often anymore, he wished he had died on that field at Waterloo. These days he didn't wish it as often mainly because he'd found a way to live with what he was, a way to justify his existence beyond the merely predatory.

But he'd seen himself reflected in Terri's blue eyes out there, and he didn't like what he saw. He was a monster. A controlled monster, but still a monster.

He put his arm over his hypersensitive eyes, shielding them from the little bit of light that trickled through two doors from the outer office. Over the past few decades or so, he thought he'd come to terms with the way things were. He'd found a kind of peace with the self-control he'd practiced for well over a hundred years. He'd even learned to live comfortably in a constant state of need. He'd stopped pining endlessly for the things he wanted but felt he couldn't morally take.

He'd reached a compromise he could live with.

And then he looked into one woman's eyes and knew that no amount of self-control could change his nature, or make him anything but what he was: monstrous.

"Jude?"

Terri's tentative voice made him lift his arm and look toward the doorway. He was actually surprised she had come this close. "Yes?"

"Can I come in?"

And torment him some more with her exquisite scent, her incredible beauty? "Sure." He deserved the torments of the damned, he supposed.

She stepped in. "Will the door lock if I close it?"

"Yes, but you can still get out. It may prevent anyone from getting in here during daylight hours, but it doesn't prevent anyone from leaving."

She turned and closed the heavy vault door. The locks automatically thunked into place, but simply pressing down the bar that served as a handle on the inside would open it. And whether she realized it or not, he had just handed her a way to kill him.

She stepped closer, and her luscious aroma began to perfume the air around him. Not that it had ever entirely dissipated.

"I'm sorry, Jude."

"For what?"

"For making you feel bad. I know I did. I was just…shocked."

"You have every right to feel shocked."

"Maybe." She came closer until finally she stood beside him. She stared down at him, and he could hear her heart begin to beat heavily.

Hunger rose in him, a force of nature he couldn't prevent himself from feeling. Instead, he chose to remain perfectly still, for fear that if he let himself move even the least bit, he might do something he would never forgive himself for.

"I'm amazed," she said.

"At what?"

"At how you can control yourself. I've been thinking about it some more and I realized… you're amazing."

"Actually, I'm a despicable monster."

"No. You're not. You could be, but you're

not. And that makes you amazing. So, I'm sorry."

"You never have to apologize to me for having a human reaction to the fact that I'm not human. Trust me, I know what I am. And I know how most humans feel about it. Or would if they believed I exist."

"Vampires are quite popular in fiction."

"That's the point, isn't it? Fiction. Reality is altogether different."

"Yes."

Waves of hesitancy emanated from her. And damned if he knew what the right thing to do would be. Reach for her? Let her stand there until she made up her mind in some way?

He just knew that having her this close was driving him nuts. Well, he should be used to that feeling by now, shouldn't he? And what the hell was he doing in here with the door closed when he was supposed to be watching over Chloe? He sat up abruptly, swinging his feet to the floor.

Terri stepped back.

"I'm supposed to be keeping an eye on Chloe. I need to ward the office."

"Ward?"

"Protect it." Glad of some task to do besides think about himself, think about Terri, think about all the dark and unpleasant things that were so inextricably part of his life, he went to open the door.

And once outside, he began to sprinkle holy water around the office, creating an unbroken circle of protection. Then he went into his office and returned with a cruet.

"What's that?" Terri asked.

"Holy oils. Father Dan gave them to me." Putting a little on his thumb, he walked around to trace a cross on every door, over every window, and on the walls for good measure.

"This stuff really holds off demons?" she asked.

"Remember what I told you about belief and faith? Yes, it works. Faith has power, Terri. Great power."

"I guess it does. I mean, I should know that already from what happened to me."

"That should keep it out," he said when he finished. "At least until Garner arrives and crosses it. I'll leave him a note to pour more holy water across the doorway."

"You mean it's only good until it's crossed?"

"No. But it can be smudged. If he steps on it and carries it to some other part of the room, there'll be an opening."

"So now Chloe is safe?"

He nodded. "She should be." He glanced at the clock as he felt his neck prickle warningly. "I don't have much time."

"Do you hate that?"

"Sometimes. Especially times like now. I'm useless during daylight hours."

"Nothing can wake you?"

"Very little. I'm dead, Terri. Or as close to it as to make no difference. I got carted off to the morgue a little over forty years ago."

"My God! Really?"

He had to smile. "Yes, really. I thought I was in a safe place, but apparently not safe enough. I assume they must have put me in a body bag before they moved me, or I wouldn't be here to tell you about it. Obviously, I'll never know exactly what happened, but when I resurrected

I was lying in a locker in the morgue with a sheet over me and a toe tag on."

"How in the world did you get out?"

"Those lockers aren't exactly designed to keep something from escaping. You should have seen the look on the attendant's face when I bashed my way free. Almost as priceless as when I took his clothes."

Terri giggled, and he was glad to hear the sound. It meant she was getting past the latest shock he had dealt her.

"That couldn't have happened here," she said. "A story like that would become legend and I'd have heard about it."

"Not here. I have to move every ten years or so because people will notice I'm not aging."

She sat on the couch. "I never thought about that."

"Why would you? You age normally."

"What about the rest of it?" she asked. "Does your reflection show in a mirror?"

"I'm a vampire, not a ghost. I don't understand that lame-brained notion. For you to be able to even see me, I have to reflect light."

"True. The same for photographs?"

"Same answer."

"And obviously you don't turn into a bat."

"There are shapeshifters, but I'm not one of them."

That caught her. He enjoyed watching the wheels spin behind her blue eyes, so he leaned back against Chloe's desk and folded his arms, waiting for the next question, curious as to what it might be.

"Umm, okay, you did say shapeshifters?"

"I did."

"Vampires?"

"Not us, no. But there are other beings out there. And whatever form they happen to be in at the time, you'd never notice them."

"Like werewolves?"

"Definitely, although the modern passion for exterminating wolves has reduced their numbers. You should read shamanic tradition sometimes. Shapeshifting rests at its core. Shamans take on the form of various animals at times. And then there are those for whom it is part of their natures. They're born able to transform themselves. And like vampires, they keep it very much secret."

"Okay, you're rocking my world again."

"I thought that might. This would be a good time to quote one of Shakespeare's most famous lines, but I'll spare you since I'm sure you already know it. Just take my word for it, there's a lot about the world that you don't know simply because you're not invited to see it."

She nodded, a thoughtful nod. "I guess I have a lot to learn."

"Most of it you probably won't ever need to know about or deal with. Those of us who live in the shadows generally prefer to remain in them."

He glanced at the clock again, confirming what his neck was telling him.

"You're going to sleep soon," she remarked.

"Yes. Unfortunately."

She looked at him, steadily, and then he smelled it: more than her intoxicating scent, the heady aroma of burgeoning desire. She wanted him again. And time was so short now that he figured it might be safe to give her what she wanted.

Because he wanted to give it to her. He

needed to give it to her, if for no other reason that it would prove she hadn't come to find him repulsive. He was amazed at how much it pained him to think that she might.

Most of the time, he didn't care what anyone else thought of him. All that mattered was what he thought of himself, and oftentimes those thoughts were dark and ugly.

But the reflection of himself that he saw now in Terri's eyes was entrancing. She had accepted him just as he was. Even that ugly part about being attracted to fear. If she had not, she couldn't possibly be looking at him the way she was now.

As if he were a feast and she was as hungry for him as he for her.

She rose and closed the space between them. He forced himself to utter stillness because he had to be sure, absolutely sure, that what happened next was of *her* choosing. He needed, heart and soul, to know that she came to him freely.

Unlike so many in the past.

She reached up and cupped his cheek. "I like the way you feel cool, not cold. I didn't

know I'd like that. Your skin is so smooth."
Then she slipped her hand behind his head and
pulled him toward her.

But not to her mouth. To her neck. He almost froze in shock at what she was inviting,
and squeezed his eyes shut as he battled not to
grant her wish.

His face came to rest in the hollow between
her neck and shoulder. Her heartbeat was as
loud as a drum in his ear, and his own heart
synchronized to it, inevitable now that he had
tasted her, and oh, so sweet when it happened.

He filled his lungs with her even as he refused to take what she offered. Nor could he
imagine why she was offering. "It's too soon,"
he said thickly.

Desperate to save them both from her offer
and his compulsions, he swept her off her feet
and carried her to his bedroom. With a shoulder he shoved the door closed behind them, the
sound of the lock barely piercing the drumbeat
of his/her heart in his ears.

So little time, thank God. He could give her
one part of what she wanted and then fall into

inevitable sleep before he could lose control of himself and take all that *he* wanted.

For the first time in his immortal life, he actually saw the sleep of death as a saving grace.

But something compelled him not to spare her. Not to leave her with any illusions. She wanted a vampire? Fine. He would show her at least part of what that could mean.

She had no idea, for example, that he could move fast enough to strip her naked between one breath and the next. If she felt anything at all, it was the whispering movement of air, and then she stood before him wearing nothing.

She gasped, and looked down at herself. Color stained her cheeks, and she looked up at him from beneath her lashes.

"Getting the idea?" he asked.

"What idea?"

"I could take you, make you and drink you nearly dry almost before you knew it."

She lifted her head and looked at him. "I get it."

"Good. Ready to run?"

"No."

Damn, she was stubborn. Slowing himself

down, he dragged his inky gaze over her body, enjoying her loveliness. Not perfect, but oh, so desirable, from the throbbing pulse in her throat, to just-right breasts, to hips that invited a man. Even a bit of tummy, which he found arousing despite the modern trend for women to be hollow there. To his way of thinking, no healthy woman should have a concave belly.

Legs that were nicely shaped, somehow managing to appear long despite her small size. Even the high arches of her feet seemed perfect to him, and he could easily imagine kissing her there, nibbling her there. Perhaps even biting her there.

Her nipples were large, and they hardened and pinkened under his perusal. He liked that. Smiling, he reached out and brushed his hand over one, watching the shiver course through her.

"Not fair," she whispered, reaching for the buttons of his shirt.

He brushed her hands away, and stripped himself in another instant, so that he, too, stood nude before her. Let her see that in one important way he was still a man.

Her eyes widened, but all he saw was appreciation. He forced himself to remain perfectly still as she reached out and began to run her palms over him. Ah, heavens, it was so sweet, and so long since he had allowed any woman to touch him this way. So long.

Because it had been forever since he wanted a woman as anything more than a passing fancy. Because it had been forever since he had dared share himself for fear he might lose control.

With Terri he was sure he could maintain his control, primarily because she had managed to become more important to him than his own wants and needs.

Something like a warning went off in his head, but he ignored it. He needed her touches more than he had imagined. When she wrapped her warm hand around his staff, he nearly lost it.

But self-control, long practiced, came to his rescue. In a movement too fast for her to register, but that seemed almost slow motion to him, he swept her from her feet onto his bed and lay beside her.

She gasped, then giggled, surprising him. An instant later she had clasped his face in her hands and drew him close for another kiss. He very nearly inhaled her sweet breath from her lungs. God, it had been so long since he had allowed himself to want like this. To need like this.

He had to school himself to move slowly, to run his hands all over her at a speed she could enjoy. When she reciprocated he shuddered with a longing as intense as any he had ever felt. It had been too long since he had permitted a woman to make love to him in return. Control had a high price, and he'd long since schooled himself not to risk losing it at any cost.

But something had changed. Exactly what, he couldn't say, except that somewhere deep within himself he knew he wouldn't hurt Terri no matter what. He was sure of it.

So he relished her warm hands as they explored him, teasing him gently, then less so, as if she wanted her palms and fingers to memorize every inch of him.

He gave in to the desire to learn her the

same way, enchanted as much by the warmth of her body as by its delicious curves and hollows. Warmth. God, he craved the warmth of a human being. It was the only warmth that could reach him anymore, raising hunger and desire to heights of near ecstasy.

"Do I feel too cold to you?" he asked, out of awareness of how warm she felt to him.

"No," she whispered. "Oh, no. Cool, not cold. Not at all cold." Then, a soft giggle. "I'm hot enough for both of us."

He stole her breath in a kiss, then proceeded to nibble, just nibble, his way along her body, never breaking the skin, but soothing, if not salving, a need of his own. When he felt her response, a shudder ran through him, too.

He had tasted her blood. Having tasted it, the bond it created doubled his experience. He felt every trip of her heart as if it were his own. He smelled the rising scents of desire, almost seemed to feel the tingles running along her nerve endings as well as his. When he at last reached that exquisite bundle of nerves between her legs, he showed her that the faintest hint of pain could excite her even more.

Damn, he wanted to give in to his every need, but care for her prevented him. His heart thundered with hers. His breaths became gasps. His loins clenched with a hunger of their own, equal to his other hunger, the one he dared not give in to.

The sound of his name emerging from her lips on a moan almost crazed him. He couldn't remember the last time he had wanted sex so badly. In his life, it had come to take second place to a darker need. Until now. Until this woman.

Rising over her, settling between her parted legs, he plunged into her. Her hot wet depths received him. He groaned and almost lost it.

But at the last second, he found a shred of control, grabbing a pillow and turning his head to the side. He bit into the pillow as he pumped again and again, rising ever higher on the tide of need, until he felt her shudder of completion.

Then he joined her, his teeth piercing a pillow, his body piercing hers.

Heaven could hardly offer more.

Chapter 12

"We can't stay in a bunker!"

The sounds of the quarrel reached Jude as soon as he emerged from his vault. Terri had slipped out a few minutes earlier, after showering, and he had waited to take his own shower.

Dark things rode his shoulders now, and he couldn't afford the inevitable distraction if he had showered with Terri. He had gone to places with her that he had not gone to with a woman in a long, long time, and even an immortal could get impatient to repeat such joys.

He walked through his office and stepped out into the outer office where the quarreling was going on between Chloe, Garner and evidently even Terri.

"Garner," Chloe said, "you don't know what we're up against here. Don't be an idiot."

Garner, who was pacing rather feverishly, threw up a hand. "So we stay locked in here surrounded by holy water and holy oil? What is that going to solve? We can't let this thing keep doing this!"

"I agree," Terri said. Her blue eyes seemed to snap. "We're virtual prisoners here. This can't go on. I've got to get back to work, for one thing."

Jude stood in the doorway wondering what had brought this on. Last night Terri had been frightened, and today she wanted to follow a hare-brained Garner's suggestions?

"Am I allowed to join the discussion?" he drawled, allowing just a hint of sarcasm to creep into his voice.

At once Terri looked at him, and he saw the faint pink stain on her cheeks. Damn, that called to him.

"Garner's being an idiot again," Chloe said. "He doesn't even know what we're dealing with here and he wants to charge off and go hunting for it. And Terri must have lost her mind to even suggest it. What did you do to her?"

"I didn't do a damn thing." At least nothing that she hadn't wanted as much as he had. "Terri? I know what Garner's thinking. He always wants to take the bull by the horns. But what are you thinking?"

"That this thing could outwait us forever. That there's no way we can hunker down indefinitely. We have lives to lead. So we have to go after it, somehow."

He folded his arms and leaned against the doorjamb looking at three people who had become so important in his existence. To his very core he knew he would protect them with his life, if he could call it that. Yet, protecting them did not include keeping them locked up forever.

The question was how to handle this. "If we separate we might become weaker," he said. "But if we don't, we may never get rid of the threat."

Chloe put her hands on her hips. "Not alone you don't."

"Absolutely not." Terri sprang to her feet. "No way you're going out there alone. If you go, I go. And don't try to stop me."

"You have absolutely no idea how easily I could stop you."

She glared at him, and it pained him, but it was also the truth. Some things needed to be clear, including how implacable he could be when necessary. But apparently, he underestimated Terri.

"You may be able to stop me, but what's the point, Jude? This thing needs a wedge to get at you or Creed. It's come after me, it's gone after Creed's granddaughter. You can go out there and hunt all night every night and it won't approach you. No, it'll wait until it has a chance to get at someone you care about. So we might as well just go out there and face it. And since it's been nosing around me for a while now, I'd make the best bait."

He closed his eyes. The pain he felt at her words was both unanticipated and sharper than a dagger. "I can't risk you," he said.

"You won't get it any other way. And I'm going to have to go out there, anyway. I have a job, remember? You're not seriously proposing we live the rest of our lives, all of us, inside these walls?"

"I need to think. There has to be another way."

"If you can come up with one, fine. But I've been doing a lot of thinking while you slept, and I can't see any other way."

Everyone remained still and silent for several seconds, then Chloe shocked them all by hurling a pencil across the room. Jude's eyes snapped open.

"This stinks," she said. "This reeks." Then she jabbed a finger at Jude. "I told you you needed to teach us all. I *told* you."

"Yes. You did."

"You should have let me call Father Dan."

"Maybe so. Maybe so." Then he turned and went back into his office, determined to find a different solution from the one Terri was proposing. She didn't know the risks. She couldn't begin to understand the risks.

He suspected she was behind the mini revolution taking place out there. Chloe would never dream up such a scheme, and Garner, for all he always wanted to get involved, rarely came up with a new idea of his own that made any real sense.

No, Terri was the force behind this storm. And that was troubling indeed.

"Garner!"

The young man materialized instantly in the doorway.

"Come in and shut the door."

Garner hastened to obey. "I swear it wasn't my idea, man," he said immediately. "But I think she's right."

"I know it wasn't your idea."

"Oh." The young man looked relieved. Then, "How can you know it wasn't my idea?"

"Trust me, you don't want to know."

"Oh." Garner shifted, clearly unsure how to take that. "So what do you want me to do?"

"Do you smell it around her?"

Garner's blond brows both lifted. "No way, man. If I did, I'd be all over it."

"Pay attention. Keep sensing."

"I can do that."

Moments later, Jude sat alone again. Had he been mortal, he was sure he would have been sweating with fear.

When Jude didn't emerge from his office for a while after sending Garner out, Terri decided to go face the lion in his lair. She couldn't stand being on edge, couldn't stand the thought he might be angry with her, could tolerate even less being away from him.

But they had to solve this somehow.

He looked up when she opened the door and stepped in. "Go away," he growled. "I need to think."

"Are you mad at me?"

"I said I needed to think!" He thundered the words, and it was all she could do not to quail. But she stood her ground, anyway. This was the vampire who had bitten a pillow last night rather than give in to his overwhelming desire to bite her. He didn't frighten her anymore. Not at all.

"No," she answered sharply. "You listen to me, Jude Messenger. We're all in this mess now. You can't just come hide in here and make decisions for all of us."

"None of you truly understands what we're up against. Damn it, Terri, I need time and space to figure this out."

"I've got a pretty good idea what we're up against. Enough to know that thing is going to use me against you, whether today, tomorrow or next month."

"I know." His tone was heavy, and the eyes that stared back at her were black as night. "Do you think I don't realize that? I fell right into its trap. I not only wanted you, but I came to care for you. Too much!"

She gasped. "Jude…"

"It's been almost two hundred years since the last time my gut twisted in terror. And now it's twisting because of you. You're bait, and I'm well into the trap."

She felt her color drain, and she sagged into the chair beside the door. "I'm sorry," she whispered. She felt light-headed, and more distressed that she could have imagined possible. She had brought him to this. "I don't want you to live in terror. I'll just leave. Ignore whatever happens to me."

"Damn it, Terri! Damn it all to bloody hell. You don't get it. I'm not terrified for myself. I care damn all what happens to me. It's *you* I'm worried about. You're the reason my insides are twisting in terror. And this terror is worse that any I ever knew in battle. I can't let anything happen to you."

"Oh." Now she felt excessively small. She gazed down at her twisting hands, wondering what she could possibly say that would ease his concern even the slightest.

"Oh," he said bitterly, "it baited the trap beautifully. It must have sensed my reaction to your scent and then sent those thugs after you so that I would have to come to your aid. Otherwise, I'd have walked away."

She bit her lip and closed her eyes, absorbing the blows as they came.

"I knew you were dangerous," he said. "I just didn't know *how* you'd be dangerous. I thought all I had to worry about was losing my control with you. Then I thought I couldn't maintain it, anyway, because damn it, I wanted you so much, and every time I sent you away you came back and I wanted you even more. You were the lure and I didn't even know it."

Terri's heart squeezed painfully, and the air seemed to have become too thick to draw into her lungs. "So," she finally asked, when she could get a breath, "I'm just a lure?"

"To that *thing,* yes. But not to me. Not now. No, you're much more to me than that. Which is what it wanted. It went after Creed through his granddaughter, but we kept Creed from hunting it alone. Maybe it thought that if Creed asked for my help we'd go out there and do something stupid. I don't know. But I *do* know that it's achieved its goal. It has a wedge to use on me now. A huge one. And now you, that very wedge, want to walk out of here and take it head-on? I don't think so, Terri."

"But…"

"Don't give me any *but*s. If that thing possesses you, it could decide to hold you long enough to kill you. It wouldn't take long for it to sap you."

"But you can exorcise it!"

"What if I can't? I've never dealt with this

sort of demon before. If I get it out of you, that doesn't necessarily make it gone, the way it is with weaker demons. This one can just keep hopping around and come back for another strike. But I am sure as hell not going to risk letting it kill you."

"If it…it tries to kill me, you can turn me, right?"

He swore savagely.

Terri felt her insides go weak. "Jude?"

"If I drink from you when you're possessed, it will get exactly what it wants. Me."

"Oh." Her usually clear mind was now running in crazy circles, trying to make any kind of sense out of this and failing.

"That is why, job or no job, you're not leaving this office until I figure out something. Because we're in a box, Terri. It *will* get one of us if we don't know exactly what we're doing."

"But I fought it off once before. I drove it away. Maybe it can't possess me. Maybe I can still fight it off."

"At this point, fighting it off will be only a temporary solution. Regardless, you're assuming that what troubled you in your childhood was the same thing. We can't know that. The only thing your childhood experience tells me is that in some way, some demon thought you might be susceptible. Clearly you weren't. To *that* demon."

"I get it." She shook her head. "Jude, I'm not stupid. Really."

"You're the furthest thing from stupid imaginable. But you're new to this world. Naive."

"Obviously." She twisted her fingers together, then forced them to relax. "I couldn't bear it if anything happened to you because of me."

"Then be patient. Please. There's something at the back of my mind, rattling around. I can't quite get to it. Something I heard or read long ago. I don't know. It might be useless regardless. But I need time and space to think, and I can't do that if I'm worrying about you darting out the door."

"I won't."

"Good."

She hesitated, then asked, "How do you turn someone? Just by drinking from them?"

"No. Of course not. But I have to drink

enough of your blood that it becomes thoroughly mixed with mine. Bring you almost to death, actually. Then I feed you myself, returning to you our mixed blood. I don't know how it works. I just know that only by passing our sufficiently mixed blood back to you can I be sure you'll resurrect."

"If you did that to me now that thing couldn't possess me."

"Terri!"

She saw the horror on his face and couldn't say she was surprised. She knew what he thought of his kind of existence. But it was the only way out she could think of. "If it comes to that…"

"I won't let it," he said harshly. "I won't. You have a proper life to live, and I'll be damned if I take it from you."

For some reason she didn't want to consider just then, that hurt. But it was obvious to her that she had nothing at all to offer. All her education and apparently even her experience were useless now. So at last she rose to leave the room, but even as she was turning to the door, Jude was suddenly there in front of her.

He cupped her neck and chin gently with one hand and bent to kiss her. "Please," he said, "don't think I'm angry with you. I'm not. I'm angry with myself."

"No need." She looked up into his dark-as-night eyes, and despite everything felt the trickle of longing he never failed to awake in her. "This is not your fault. It's no one's fault. I'll leave you to think."

Just a few minutes after she returned to the outer office, joining Chloe and Garner in glum preoccupation, Jude called out. "Chloe? Get me the grimoire, please."

"Jude!" Chloe sounded appalled.

Jude instantly appeared in the doorway of his office. "If you won't get it for me, then I will."

Chloe jumped up and stood in front of the wall behind her desk where a large painting hung. "Touching that thing scares me. You had me lock it up for a reason."

"Yes, because of how it might be used. But I need it now."

Chloe shook her head. "The dark arts are never the answer."

"They are when you need to find a weakness." He reappeared in front of her. "Move to the side, please. I'd rather not move you myself."

Chloe's lips set, but she stepped out of the way. Jude swung the painting away from the wall, revealing a safe. He worked the combination almost too fast to see, then opened it to remove a very old, very thick book.

He closed up the safe, moved the picture back into place, then turned to Chloe again. "Call Creed. Ask him to get over here quickly. I may have remembered something and I need him."

Then he was gone again. Chloe sat down at her desk, scratched impatiently at her forehead, and looked as if someone had told her the world was about to end. "Call Creed," she said, wagging her head in disapproval, her tone snitty. "Yeah, I'll call Creed. Maybe he has some sense left."

"What's a grimoire?" Terri asked.

"You don't want to know. But if your curiosity is killing you, look it up online. In the meantime, I'm supposed to be calling Creed."

It was a strangely subdued Garner who answered her. "It's a book of magic spells. For summoning demons and angels, supposedly. Or other things."

Terri felt ice water trickle down her spine. It sounded like a book she would never even want to open the cover on.

Who the hell would want to summon a demon?

"It also," Garner said, "tells you how to get rid of them when you're done with them. Of course, that's the tricky part."

"Tricky?"

"Demons and djinns and things like that often want a little *quid pro quo*. But I doubt Jude is going to ask a demon to do anything for him. He's just looking for a way to send this one back."

Another icy chill trickled through her. "I'd be afraid to even read the book. And I don't think I'm superstitious."

"Oh, it's got nothing to do with superstition," Chloe said, phone to her ear. "This is *real*. Why else do you think Jude keeps that book in a safe? Hi, Creed. Jude needs you now.

I don't know what he wants, but maybe you can talk some sense into him."

Jude's voice issued from the inner office. "I heard that."

"Not my fault you don't like what I say. Creed heard you, too, by the way. He's laughing. Thanks, Creed," she said and hung up.

"Laughing," Chloe said, disgust dripping from the word. "Only vampires could find this amusing."

"I heard that, too," Jude called out. "Trust me, Chloe, I am not in the least amused by any of this."

Chloe sniffed, but fell silent.

Terri simply didn't know what to say or even think. This was all so far outside the familiar that she just kept drawing big blanks.

Only Garner appeared to remain confident. "Jude will figure this out."

Terri sure hoped so.

Creed arrived little more than twenty minutes later. He looked far happier than when she had last seen him. "Is your granddaughter better?"

"Much so. Improving by leaps and bounds, physically. She'll probably need therapy, though." His face darkened at that.

Terri hesitated then asked, "Does she know about you?"

"No. Of course not. She's never even met me."

Terri felt a pang. "That's sad, Creed. But you keep an eye on her?"

"Yes, I do. I may not be much of a guardian angel, but I do what I can. Too bad I wasn't watching over her the other night."

"Nobody can watch someone else every minute of the day."

"Not even a vampire, unfortunately. But she'll mend, thank God."

Jude called out from his office again. "Creed?"

"Coming." Creed looked down at Terri and smiled faintly. "You're amazing, for a mortal. I rather like you, Dr. Black."

Then he disappeared swiftly into Jude's office, closing the door behind him.

Terri looked at Chloe. "What did that mean? Amazing for a mortal?"

Chloe shrugged. "Maybe that you seem to be taking the undead in stride?"

For some reason Terri felt a crazy urge to giggle. "In my job I deal with the dead all the time. Undead is only a step removed."

Chloe finally let go of her disapproval and relaxed into a grin. "But ever so much more trouble!"

An hour later, Jude and Creed emerged from the inner sanctum. Something in Jude's step immediately told Terri he was feeling confident again. At least more confident than earlier.

"Okay," he announced as he went to the safe and put the grimoire safely back inside. "Here's what's going to happen."

"I can hardly wait," Chloe muttered.

"Chloe, you're going to that shop you know over on West Alma."

"The place that sells all that stuff for potions?"

"Exactly. I need you to do some specialized shopping. They close at midnight, right?"

"Or later, but yeah."

"Creed is going with you for protection. He has a list of the things I need. I want exactly those things."

"I can do that," Chloe agreed. "What are you going to do?"

"Some things you don't need to know about." He ignored Chloe's huff of displeasure. "Creed?"

"Let's go," Creed said to Chloe. "Limited time."

"All right, all right." Chloe grabbed her purse and held out her hand to Jude. He put a credit card in it.

"Everything," he repeated. "Exactly."

"I can follow orders."

"When you choose."

Jude watched them leave then turned to Garner. "Go out and test the night, Garner. Especially down by the warehouse district. It's out there. If you catch a whiff, report back immediately."

Garner leapt up, clearly glad there was something to do besides sit around.

And then Terri was alone with Jude. He sat beside her on the couch, and took her hand, his touch cool. "I hope you're brave," he said.

"Do I have any choice?"

"It doesn't look like it."

"Then I'm brave. What are we doing?"

"I'm going to set a trap to send that thing back to hell. You have to promise to do exactly what I say, no matter what. We're messing with dangerous stuff tonight."

"Black arts?" She only had a foggy idea of what such things could be.

"Something like. It's going to be risky. It might fail."

She nodded, pressing her lips together, feeling her heart begin to hammer. "I'm going to face that thing?"

"You're the lure. But I'm the real bait. It doesn't want you except as a way to get to me. So we're going to set a trap, and you're going to do exactly what I say, and you're going to pray as hard as you've ever prayed. I'm going to give you some incantations to read. You must read them exactly the way they're written, and you must do it exactly when I tell you."

"I can do that."

"I know you can." He reached out, running

a cool fingertip over her cheek, and along her jawline. "It's too late, Terri."

Her heart slammed. "Too late? What's too late?"

"We'll talk later. If I don't succeed tonight, it won't even matter."

"What? Jude, please!"

He leaned forward to silence her with a kiss. "Just know this, sweet one," he whispered. "No matter what happens, you hold a place in my heart that no one ever has."

She gave in then, bringing up her arms to wrap them around his neck, drawing him close, letting him press his face into the hollow of her throat, hoping he might take her blood there and then because she felt such a need, such a deep and overwhelming need, to give him what he most craved.

Instead, she felt featherlight kisses on her throat, felt him inhale her scent deep into his lungs. Then he sighed and straightened, looking deep into her eyes.

"When I am close to you now, my heart keeps time with yours."

A ripple of pleasure poured through her. "Really?"

He kissed her cheek then drew back. "Really. And if I keep this up we'll be otherwise engaged when the rest return. First we deal with this *thing*. Then we'll deal with us."

She liked that word, *us*. A different kind of shiver ran through her as she wondered if they'd both still be around come dawn. Leaning forward, she rested her head against his shoulder and sent a prayer winging heavenward that they would both survive the night.

Somehow, from what she knew of Jude, she didn't think heaven would object to such a prayer at all.

When Creed and Chloe returned with a large shopping bag, Jude emptied it, examining its contents. There seemed to be herbs, incense sticks, candles and even a large lighter, and a box of chalk.

"Perfect, Chloe."

"I told you I can follow orders. Now what are you going to do with that?"

"Trick a demon."

"Sounds like a great plan."

"There is no other plan." Jude put everything in the bag. "Time's wasting. Terri, come with me. I want to explain to you what's going to happen, then we'll go."

She followed him into his office again, her feet leaden. Why did she think she wasn't going to like any of this?

Jude closed the door firmly and waved her to a chair. He sat behind his desk as if he was determined to keep a distance between them. "Ready?" he asked.

"As I'll ever be."

"This isn't going to make you happy."

"I didn't think it would."

He gave her a half smile. "You're the lure."

"You said that already."

"Ah, but you're also the lure for that demon. You attract it as surely as you attract me."

"I didn't even think of that!"

"For different reasons, but you lure it the same as you lure me. So we're going to use that."

"Okay. That's what I was saying earlier, basically."

"Basically. But this time we're going to be ready, prepared. And you're not going to like it."

"We already covered that. What do I need to do?"

"I found a way we may be able to send it back to hell. But first we have to localize it."

Terri didn't need a translation. "You mean it has to occupy me."

"Or me. If it occupies you, I'll attempt to exorcise it. If that doesn't work, I may have to grant it permission to possess me."

"Jude, no!"

"Terri, yes. Just listen. That thing wants *me* not only because I'm immortal, but because I have the innate ability to become a terror beyond your imagining. If that thing takes me over, it can wreak horror I don't even want to describe. *That's* why it wants a vampire."

She nodded, going almost numb with fear. "But if it takes you…"

"Then we have to stop it at any cost. *Any* cost, Terri. Even if it means killing me."

She jumped up. "No!"

"Terri, listen to me."

"No, I'm not going to kill you. I'm not going to stand by while someone else kills you!"

"Terri..." An instant later he was there, his arms wrapped tightly around her, steel bands she could not escape.

"Listen to me. *Listen to me!*"

Finally she nodded, even though she could feel the sting of tears in her eyes.

"You cannot conceive what I am capable of. Unleashed and misdirected I could instill such terror in this city that people would be afraid to emerge from their locked houses. I could do that. I could go on a killing rampage that would approach genocide. I could leave such a bloody trail behind me that you humans would never feel safe again. And little could stop me. Do you think I want to become that monster? I would rather die."

She bit her lip so hard she tasted blood. She saw his eyes darken, knew he smelled it and wanted it, and much as she wished she could drive his words from her mind, make herself forget them, she knew he wasn't exaggerating. The little she had seen of his capabilities was enough to verify the truth. He *could* become a monster beyond reckoning.

"But I can be killed," he said flatly. "I can be. The sunlight. Fire. Decapitation. Those things can kill me. The demon knows this and will try to avoid it. It wants me as I am, not dead."

Still biting her lip, feeling a hot tear roll down her cheek, she nodded. Speech seemed impossible.

"So here is the thing. If it takes you and I fail to exorcise you, I'll invite it to take me. If that happens, you're going to wake up in the midst of things, because while you're possessed, you won't remember anything from when the demon is in control. If you become suddenly aware that things have changed, then you must presume I am possessed. Don't trust me. I'm going to make a protective circle. If the demon holds me, it cannot cross the unbroken circle."

Again she nodded, trying to take every word to heart.

"It may try to break the circle, scuff it if it's pretending to be me, so that once it enters it can still escape. If that happens, you must immediately close the circle."

"How?"

"I'll show you when I make it. If I refuse to enter the circle, use fire. Every bit of fire you can. Burn me if necessary. Drive me into it, and seal it."

"Burn you?" She quailed at the thought.

"I can heal from any burn except immolation. The demon won't want to risk that. So burn me if you must to get me into the circle. Then you must do and say exactly what I've written down for you. Exactly. Can you do that, Terri? Can you?"

She closed her eyes a moment, drawing a shaky breath, facing all the he had told her and the consequences of not obeying. In the end it was the thought of many lives that might be lost if she failed that persuaded her. The thought of Jude being turned into something he loathed. She opened her eyes. "I can."

He studied her for several seconds, then nodded. "Okay. We'll go as soon as Garner gets something."

Chapter 13

"It's near."

An hour later Terri and Jude were in the warehouse district, entering an abandoned brick building filled with dust, rats and discarded trash. Jude hadn't worn his usual leather coat, but instead a linen jacket. She suspected, with a sick and heavy heart, that he had chosen the jacket for its flammability.

"How do you know?" she asked. The darkness frightened her, pierced only by their flashlights, the huge echoing space seemed full of threat.

"I smelled it. I know the scent now. It's not here yet, but we passed it."

Faster than she could see, he cleared a space on the cement floor. His movements were so quick that they stirred the dust up into choking clouds. Her heart hammered, feeling as if it had risen into her throat.

Then Jude approached, took the flashlight from her and set it on the floor. "I'm going to tie you to that pillar."

"But how can I help if I can't move?" Her mouth seemed to have turned into the Sahara.

"Only until I make the circle. In case it arrives early, I don't want it to be able to stop me. Believe me, I'll untie you as soon as I deem it wise."

She licked her lips and walked over to the concrete post nearby. Leaning her back against it, she closed her eyes and said the St. Michael prayer silently as she felt ropes wind around her, snug but not too tight.

"Don't pray too hard," Jude said humorously. "We don't want to keep it away, remember?"

"This is not funny!"

"No," he agreed. "It's not. Just trying to cheer you up. If it makes you feel better, keep praying until I'm done making the circle."

She did exactly that, but watched intently because she realized she might be called upon to close that circle if things went awry.

He spoke as he worked. "I'm not going to close it just yet. If it possesses me, you're going to have to be able to force me into this circle. No demon can cross this circle once it's closed, whatever the provocation. However, as long as you're not possessed, and I'm not possessed, we can cross that circle simply by stepping over it. But don't step on the lines or smudge them."

He drew a large circle with chalk. Inside it, he drew a pentagram, ensuring that the corners touched the edges of the circle. "Depending on direction," he said, "this can be protective or demonic."

"How's that?"

"Upside-down it can be interpreted at a horned goat. Right side up it signifies the crucifixion."

"How do you know which is which?"

"North is considered up."

She watched uneasily as he drew it upside-down. "Why are you making the goat then?"

"Because it's hell I want to open a gate to."

Her skin began to crawl, and the room seemed to be growing colder. Just her imagination, she told herself. Nothing but imagination.

At each point of the star, he placed a thick, tall candle and lit it. Outside, he arranged the incense sticks in small holders and started them all burning. Then just outside the circle, he lay some bound, dried herbs.

"Sage," he said. "With a few other powerful herbs mixed in. I don't know why, but demons tend to find sage smoke utterly repellant. If I get possessed, light it and wave it everywhere, but stay outside the circle." Then he held up the wand lighter and struck it, adjusting it so that a large flame shot from its tip. "Use this against me if you have to, to force me inside the circle, and don't be afraid to set my clothes afire. That demon won't want me immolated any more than I do."

"Jude…"

"Promise me."

She swallowed, hard to do when her mouth was so dry, and nodded. "I promise."

"Remember, if it doesn't kill me, I'll recover. If it does kill me, the world will be safe regardless. So just do it, Terri."

"I promised."

He came toward her, brushing a cool kiss on her lips. "Don't hesitate. All it needs is hesitation."

Then he stepped, walked back to the circle and set some folded papers on a nearby box. "Those are the incantations. You don't have to understand them, just mean them."

"How can I do that if I don't understand?"

"All you need to know is that they are meant to drive a demon back to hell, so mean them with your whole heart."

"Okay." She was shivering now, from both fear and cold. How had it grown so cold?

"When you close the circle," he said, pointing to an area he hadn't chalked in, "use blood." He lifted a plastic bottle from the bag he'd brought. "This blood contains chrism, holy oil."

She watched as he trailed it carefully around the entire circle he had drawn. And with every drop of blood hitting the chalk line, she felt the room grow colder. That feeling of being watched began to overwhelm her.

Then she felt nothing at all.

She woke suddenly, unbound and found herself standing outside the circle. Had the exorcism succeeded? God, she felt as if she had been beaten, as if her insides had been turned to ice.

Jude, where was Jude?

She turned and saw him standing to one side, smiling. "It worked?"

"Oh, definitely," he said, looking quite pleased with himself. "It's gone."

But just as instant relief started to wash through her, she felt it again. Scared beyond words, she took a tentative step toward Jude and the feeling grew stronger.

It was still here.

"Jude?"

"I told you everything's fine."

Then why couldn't she believe him? She

hesitated, even though she had been warned not to. "Then we can go home?"

"Of course. It's gone."

"I guess I should gather everything up."

"Don't bother. We don't need it anymore."

And something was very definitely not right. The Jude she knew should seem happier if the exorcism had succeeded, and less self-satisfied. If there was one thing she knew about Jude, he was never self-satisfied. But right now he reeked of it.

"I just hate to leave a mess." Shaking, but hoping it didn't show, she walked over and picked up the papers. Then the lighter.

"Really," he said. "We don't need that."

That was when she realized he was right behind her. She struck the lighter, causing flame to shoot from it, and turned to face him. "Don't come near me."

"You wouldn't hurt me, love."

And he'd never called her that. God, it was Jude yet not Jude. For an instant her mind froze, then all the directions came hurtling back. "Then get inside the circle."

"Why would I do that?"

"To prove yourself."

"Don't be ridiculous, Terri. It's me."

She drew a deep steadying breath, aware that she had to act, and act now. Jude had told her what to do.

With the eight-inch flame still shooting from the tip of the wand lighter, she waved it close to him.

"Fire kills you," she said. "And I'm not opposed to killing a vampire. Get in that circle."

He laughed. "Oh, all right."

She watched him pass through the open part of the arc then turn to face her.

"See?" he said. Then he started to walk toward her again.

"Stop!"

"Terri, don't be silly."

Jude. She had to save Jude from this thing somehow. And that thought brought fury to her rescue. A woman had nearly been killed by this thing. It wanted free reign to murder and terrorize. No, this was not Jude she was looking at right now, and that realization gave her strength.

As he approached, she jabbed the lighter

across the circle, catching the sleeve of his linen jacket. The linen ignited immediately, and she saw his eyes widen. He started patting out the flame, but it was spreading faster than he could put it out.

With her other hand, she grabbed the bottle of blood and chrism, and barely daring to take her eyes from Jude, she closed the circle.

"Ah, you shouldn't have done that," the demon said.

She stepped back, quickly checking for any other breaks in the circle. She could see none.

She grabbed the sage bundles and lit them, watching thick smoke start to rise.

"Terri, you're burning me."

That cry sounded so much like a human in pain that her heart stuttered and she almost, almost gave in. But when she looked at the demon again, she saw that he'd nearly put the fire out. Nearly.

"Why are you treating me this way?" he demanded. "I thought we had something special."

Any lingering doubt vanished with that. Jude would have known exactly why she was doing this. He'd even been willing to be immolated, burned alive, rather than let that thing free.

Standing there holding a bundle of smoking sage and a lighter that could go out at any minute, she began to feel desperate. She needed to read those incantations, but her hands were full.

"Terri, you're a doctor," he said. "You took an oath not to do harm."

"There are levels of harm."

"And you think I'm worse? You know me. You know how hard I try to be decent."

Jude never would have said that, either. Conviction grew as hard as cement.

Something moved her then, though she knew not what. Maybe there were guardian angels, perhaps at some level she knew something unconsciously. Bending, she placed the smoking sage so that it just touched the circle of blood and chrism. Blood wouldn't burn well, but there was no telling how much oil Jude had put in it.

Then she stepped back, the lit electric match still in hand and watched. And little by little a flame began to flicker and slowly follow the outline of the circle.

"Terri, are you mad?"

"Maybe so." Then she snatched up the papers and unfolded them. Nonsense syllables tracked across the printed page, or at least they seemed like nonsense to her. She started to read them aloud, remembering what Jude had told her, remembering how he had said she had to mean them.

And all she knew how to mean was that she wanted to send a demon back to hell.

As she read, fire leaped higher around the circle. Impossible fire, there was not enough there to burn like that, but higher it grew.

She heard Jude bellow something, but couldn't make it out. Glancing up from the incantation she was reading, she saw tongues of flame leaping toward him.

"Terri, break the circle! I'll burn to death."

Feeling as if her heart were cracking, she ignored the plea, and kept reading. More loudly. More determinedly.

Then a howl of sheer anger and pain filled the warehouse, almost deafening in its intensity. She looked up again, and fire was now speeding across the pentagram, as if it were not chalk at all, and flames crawled higher. Jude stood in the very heart of the pentagram, and dear God, she could see his skin starting to blacken.

Tears began to pour down her face, making it almost impossible to read, but she kept on, chanting the meaningless syllables as loudly as she could. And when she came to the end of them, she added the St. Michael prayer, praying it with more fervor than ever before in her life.

A deafening crack sundered the air, the ground seemed to shake, and then all of a sudden, the flames were gone.

And Jude lay collapsed in the middle of the circle, clearly badly burned.

She dropped everything then and put her face in her hands, weeping as if her soul had been shredded.

Worst of all, she didn't know if she dared go to his aid, didn't know if he was still possessed. And she was terrified he might be dead. Ah, God, she wished she had died, too.

* * *

"Terri." A hoarse, parched-sounding voice.

She looked up, her face wet with tears, and saw Jude had arisen and was walking toward her. Oh, God, the burns. Oh, God, how could she have done that to anyone?

"Terri," he said again.

"How do I know it's you?" she sobbed. "How do I know?"

"Because I can cross the circle."

He did so, staggering, and then collapsed on the floor beside her. "It's gone."

"You're sure?"

"Sweet one, it's gone. And if I don't get back and get some blood soon, I'll be gone, too. Take me home."

She sniffled, dashing away tears. "Don't be silly, damn it. I'm here. Drink. As much as you need." Beyond any thought of anything other than to help him, she yanked her blouse open, baring her throat. "Take it. Please."

"Not because you feel guilty."

"No. Because you need it. Because I want you to have it. Because…" She trailed off just before she said, *I love you*. But the words seemed to hang in the air, even unspoken.

Maybe he heard them, maybe he didn't. But he lay back and pulled her toward him, until her neck rested against his mouth. She felt the cool lick of his tongue, and moments later a shadow of the passion she had felt the first time she fed him. He was weak, injured, horribly burned. Perhaps he couldn't give her what he had given her that first time.

But she didn't care. Right now all that mattered was that she was giving him life and healing. Never had she more wanted to give anything.

She felt her heart race and knew he was in danger of taking too much. But she didn't care. If he sucked her dry and turned her, that would be okay, too.

But just an instant after her heart began racing, he pulled his head away, growling, "Enough!"

Slowly, reluctantly, she drew back. And blinked in amazement. His burns were already healing, turning red instead of black. The eyes that looked up at her were golden even in this dim light.

"Let's go home," he said.

The next evening, as the sun set below the horizon, even though he could not see it in his vault, Jude jerked awake with that first painful breath. When he opened his eyes he saw Terri propped on an elbow, watching him in the dim light from a lamp across the room.

"How do you feel?" she asked.

"Better than this morning."

"You look a lot better." Reaching out, she touched his cheek, his chest, his arm. "I can hardly tell you were burned."

"I told you I'd heal."

"Yes, you did." She smiled, a beautiful smile that made him truly glad to be awaking to another night.

"But what about you?" he asked. "Did I take too much?"

"No. I'm fine, and by morning I'll be pretty much back up to normal blood volume."

He reached out and touched the two small scabs on her neck. "I shouldn't have."

"Why ever not? You needed it and I could spare it."

"Because." He closed his eyes, feeling the weight of it in his heart, in the depths of his being. It might be good, or it might turn out to be the worst thing he'd ever done.

"Because what?"

He opened his eyes and looked at her. "I have claimed you."

"Really?" She sat up, crossing her legs.

He wasn't really sure what he expected—distress, perhaps?—but she astonished him. All at once a huge smile spread over her face and she looked absolutely radiant.

"Really. It knew it was a danger, I even suspected it might have already happened, but last night…when I fed from you I knew. I claimed you. My heart will always sing with yours. My thoughts will forever follow you. If you move to an igloo in Antarctica I'll move in right next door. I'm sorry."

"Sorry? Don't you want me?"

"God, Terri, *that* was never the problem. But now you're stuck with me for the rest of your days, like it or not. Short of me committing suicide, anyway."

"I kinda like that idea."

"Of me committing suicide?"

"No, of being stuck with you forever."

He could hardly believe his ears. "Terri, you've seen how I live. You can't possibly have a normal life with me."

"Normal is overrated. All I want is you, Jude. So make me like you."

"No."

"No?" Now she frowned. "Why the heck not? I want to be with you every minute of every day, and that's going to be difficult if you don't change me."

"Difficult or not, I will not do it. I won't put you through this. If you want to be with me, you're going to have to remain a human."

He watched expressions play over her face, some happy, some not so, and he waited for her verdict.

"Well." She sighed after a minute and lay down again, placing her head on his shoulder. "There are advantages to that."

"What advantages?"

"I can still feed you."

He couldn't help it. He laughed. It was probably the happiest sound he had made in a couple of centuries. "There is that," he agreed.

Then she touched his heart deeply by asking tentatively, "Forever? You promise?"

"A claiming is forever, sweet one. You're mine now. Forever."

She sighed and turned her head to kiss his chin. "I am so happy! I love you, Jude."

"I love you, Terri."

She raised up again suddenly to look at him. "You really won't change me? Ever?"

"Well, certainly not now."

"Why not?"

"Because I want to know that you're as sure as I am. Because there's no point now in turning you into what I am."

"So you might change your mind?"

He laughed and rolled over, pinning her beneath him. "My sweet love, it's always possible. But for now I'm just going to enjoy arguing with you about it for a long time to come."

That seemed to satisfy her. Probably for a week or a month, but no longer. He'd come to recognize her quiet stubbornness and appreciate it.

But there were so many other things to appreciate as well. When he entered her with his body, he felt the synchrony of feeling begin, their hearts beating as one.

This time, he didn't bite the pillow. He bit her, adding that extra fillip to his pleasure and evidently to hers. He felt her rise against him, shuddering with the same hunger and longing.

He took no more than a teaspoon from her; it was too soon.

But that teaspoon sealed the bond even more deeply, as it would forever.

He had claimed her, indeed. But she had claimed him as well.

* * * * *

A sneaky peek at next month...

NOCTURNE™

BEYOND DARKNESS...BEYOND DESIRE

My wish list for next month's titles...

In stores from 16th March 2012:

❑ The Beholder – Connie Hall

❑ The Shadow Wolf – Bonnie Vanak

In stores from 6th April 2012:

❑ Bride of the Wolf – Susan Krinard

❑ Forever Vampire – Michele Hauf

Available at WHSmith, Tesco, Asda, Eason, Amazon and Apple

Just can't wait?

0312/

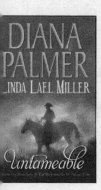

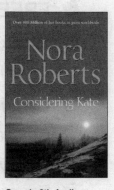